What's her Secret?

GOOD MANORS

VICTORIA BLISSE

Good Manors
ISBN # 978-1-78430-782-0

Interior text design by Claire Siemaszkiewicz
Totally Bound Publishing

Published in 2015 by Totally Bound Publishing, Newland House, The Point, Weaver Road, Lincoln, LN6 3QN, United Kingdom.

Totally Bound Publishing is a subsidiary of Totally Entwined Group Limited.

Totally Bound Publishing books by Victoria Blisse:

Sexier Side of the Hill
Travel Delight
Festive Handbag
Christmas Spirit Warms the Heart
Artistic Sights, Heavenly Delights
Tasty Italian
Switching the Control
Sweet Surrender
Sharing Nicely

Point Vamp
The Point
Stopping Point
The Vampire's Choice
The Point of Evil

The Djinn's Amulet
Silver Screen Dream
Bollywood Nightmare

Anthologies
Night of the Senses: Spiced Vanilla
Over the Moon: Moon Shy
Tempting Temps: Temporary Insanity
Whip It Up: Satisfying Desires

Collections
Merry Kinkmas: Always Christmas in Lincoln
Immortal Love: Literally Bitten
My Secret Valentine: Secret Surprise

What's her Secret?
Her Secret Past
Good Manors

GOOD MANORS

Dedication

For Matt, whose inspiration brought a new lease of life to this novel.

Chapter One

2003
India Grace

Dead, glassy eyes stared up at me from a face inhumanely pale. I recognized the corpse of Lord Mallard. On top of him a young, pert prostitute writhed, her long red nails set on his flesh above his unbeating heart. She was in the exact position she had been in when I'd snapped the lord *in flagrante* ten years ago.

There was a strange hum on the very edge of what she could hear and when I noticed the noise it grew louder and more recognizable. It was a human scream. I looked back from the prostitute's face—her eyes flat and dark, her red-ringed mouth open in fake pleasure—to the body of Lord Mallard. Fingers of ice gripped my heart, my mouth dried, I felt an overwhelming dread and when my gaze ended on the face of the corpse I saw its mouth was opened and the scream was coming from him. His eyes snapped open, his visage full of pain and accusation.

"You killed me!" he yelled, and I woke up.

I didn't have the nightmare every time I slept, like I had in the early days, but it still cropped up with regularity. Some details changed but the dead lord always accused me and I would always wake up in a cold sweat, heart thudding and my soul weighed down with guilt.

I shook my head and ran my fingers shakily through the tangle of brunette locks. It was six-fifty, ages before my alarm was set to go off.

Mondays were office days. Most of the time I worked from home or I'd be out on assignment but every Monday I went in to the *Good Manors* offices to attend meetings and pick up my latest project. Team player was definitely not my middle name but the guys in the office weren't all that bad. In fact I kind of looked forward to going in to see them.

"India, what happened? You're on time!" Brendan laughed, tugging nervously on his über-sharp gray suit lapel. I'd just walked into the reception at work.

"I was motivated by the image of your gorgeous smile, Brendan, and how today I might just get to slap it off your annoying face."

"You wound me, India Grace." Brendan flopped his long fingers back onto his forehead in a dramatic gesture.

"Not yet, but I'm working on it." I flexed my hand and pulled it into a fist. Just then Maxine, the lead editor, walked past.

"Ah, India, glad you're here. We can get on with the meeting. Lots to get through today."

"Right, Maxine, just on my way to the boardroom." I dropped my fisted hand to the side of my body and when she breezed past I poked my tongue out at Brendan, who smirked in reply. He'd won that word battle but there would always be next week. He was like an annoying younger brother—mostly I wanted to kill him but if anyone else dared pick on him I'd go straight for their jugular.

"India! Rocking the red and green combo, love."

"Thanks, Angela. Looking understatedly elegant as always."

Angela preened. She was the fashion and beauty editor of the magazine and never had a hair out of place. She could have been chased by a lion or have shagged with abandon and there wouldn't be a crease in her perfect outfit or a smear of lipstick to show it.

At first, I'd thought she was being catty when she commented on my clothes. But I'd soon found out it actually meant she liked me. I had a rather unique style. Bright clashing colors in layers almost always matched with whichever bright colored ballet shoes came to foot first. That day they were scarlet red. People who committed fashion crimes would be roundly ignored until they changed their erstwhile ways. Angela only commented on the fabulous, at least to the wearer's face.

Maxine swooped into the room, knocking the door shut and throwing a file full of paper down onto the table by her chair.

"Everyone here? Yep? Okay, we'll get started." She didn't pause to let anyone comment, just ran into her spiel without stopping. Maxine was like a teen fangirl when she got going—she barely stopped for breath even when asking someone a question. She paused for the barest second then talked over the answer. If you didn't know what to expect it was hard to deal with her unique approach to leading meetings.

Once, we'd got this new guy, Dominic Riger. He'd worked for several of the well-known high society mags and the office had been buzzing about having him with us. Unfortunately he'd only lasted one meeting with our Maxine. He was a quietly spoken well-mannered guy. Wore tweed ironically and styled his hair and mustache like a colonel in a World War I flying squad. He was smooth, he was sophisticated, but he hadn't been able to deal with Maxine and her tank-like approach to, well, everything.

He'd run out only seconds after trying to make a point and had never been seen again. The way his coat had flapped around him like the wings of a fluffed up baby bird brought a smile to my lips every time I thought about it.

I was used to Maxine's ways. People had to have a bit of a thick skin to survive at *Good Manors*. Her standards were exacting and her manner less than approachable. We were all a bit kooky and that's what set our magazine apart from the others. It was not the same old, same old.

Maxine was a creature of habit so I knew I didn't have to pay attention to her jabbering for a good while yet. It wasn't like I had a great input anyway. I was only here to get my assignment and go. Why Maxine couldn't just email me about it I didn't know. Another one of her idiosyncrasies, getting us together so she could make sure we were doing things just the way we should. The way she wanted us to.

When Angela blurted out a quick, "On it, boss," I knew it was time for me to pay attention.

"India, you were meant to be going to Bartley Manor but the gales the other night blew the roof off the guest annex, so we're sending Tom from features to cover that. I've got you a spot at Mallard Hall at short notice."

My mouth went dry, my heart raced. That was the one stately manor I couldn't possibly visit.

"But, Maxine, I've had no time to research it," I exclaimed.

She slowed mid-sentence and looked at me with something approaching contempt. "I know, but The Day in the Life article is key and you need to go somewhere. Research is overrated anyway."

"But, Maxine—"

"No buts, India. You're going. You've got the rest of the day to look it up."

And that was the end of that. No way could I interrupt again and if I did I was sure she'd simply ignore me anyway. After the meeting I commandeered a computer to look up Mallard Hall. Even typing the words made my stomach roll. I had to find a valid excuse that made sense to tell Maxine because I simply couldn't go and I couldn't tell her why that was.

I'd ruined a man's life, not just his life but that of his wife and son. I'd never be welcomed in that place. Never. As I checked out the Hall I noticed it had a snazzy new website. No longer was it just a hall—there was a farm shop, house tours, beautiful gardens and a gift shop. It had become a tourist lure.

I went to all kinds of country homes, some successful, overflowing with visitors who filled the coffers, others powered with family money, private except to me and the *Good Manors* readers. I even went to run-down places, ruins or close to, abandoned by their once owners and left to decay. I'd thought that would have been the fate for Mallard's.

I looked for connections back to the Mallard family but I couldn't find any. Flicking round, I found a promotional snippet that mentioned who was in charge at the hall.

Xander Patrick has worked passionately and single-handedly to build up the once rotting hall into a thriving visitor attraction. He introduced the farm shop in 2010, and the famous Castlemilk Moorit sheep in the last year. These innovations set Mallard Hall on the road to success.

Maybe I'd be okay. It sounded like some venture capital fellow had taken over and picked up the ruins of the old home and made it into something thriving once more.

"Oh, India, you're still here, good. I meant to give you this. It's instructions from Mallard Hall. How to get there, who to find when you arrive, that kind of thing. I'm looking forward to seeing what you write when you get back."

And off Maxine went again, her high heels clacking. She wore me out. I wondered if she ever slept or if she was just go, go, go, twenty-four-seven. I wondered briefly if she had a boyfriend but no, she surely didn't have time to slow down enough to play the seduction game. I picked up the fat brown envelope and headed for the door. Apparently I was going to be revisiting my past, and I needed to pack.

* * * *

1993

"You've got to make your name somehow, Indy. Just do it."

Lydia Dowling was my best friend and she had an annoying habit of arranging my life for me. She was also my boss.

"But, Lydia, I don't want to be in a sleazy tabloid splashing around shocking exposés. I want to do something proper."

"Oh, Indy, you silly girl. You don't get to choose, you have to go where the stories are and this is a gold-plated tip-off. Now if you're not up to the job I'm sure I can find another freelancer who'd jump at the chance—"

I was twenty-two, I'd just finished uni and I was desperate to make my way in the world. Lydia ran a journalist and photographer agency. She gave work to freelancers then sold it on to the papers, taking a cut for herself. It was a way for no-named wannabes like me to get into the press. Without Lydia, I'd have been fighting a losing battle.

"It's a good tip-off but it's messing with someone's life. He's married, isn't he?"

"Of course he's married, it wouldn't be a scandal if he wasn't!" Lydia shook her freshly rolled perm and knocked the ash off the end of her cigarette. "Look, if you want to stick to your morals I think I have a country fair that needs covering. It might get you in the local rag, I suppose. But if you really want to be noticed, this story will get you in not one but all of the nationals, I know it."

"Okay, okay, you convinced me, I'll do it."

I turned up at the Royal Standard hotel and set myself up with a view into room one-thirty-four. After just half an hour, Lord Mallard stumbled into the room with a young woman. She couldn't have been much older than me, with platinum blonde hair down to her waist, and wearing a bright pink, skintight and off the shoulder number. She held her high heels in her hand.

I couldn't hear anything as I was outside lurking in a bush. They were pretty clearly drunk. Lord Mallard lurched across the room to the minibar, pulled out a bottle and drank it in one gulp without even putting it in a glass.

It was a lot easier back then to be a pap. You could linger in bushes without fear of security teams and CCTV. It helped that the room was in the farthest corner, away from the reception. I would imagine the room had been picked purposefully to be away from the hustle and bustle so the residents could do whatever they wanted out of the way of prying eyes.

They didn't count on my eyes, though, peering through my clunky black camera. It soon became obvious that the young lady wasn't there just out of the goodness of her heart. The lord slipped his hand into his inner jacket pocket and pulled out a wodge of notes. I kept taking pictures as the money changed hands. The woman slipped the cash into her tiny handbag, threw it to the floor and her dress soon followed.

It felt weird to be watching two people engaged in such intimacies. I didn't like it. I'd always had a love of taking photos and playing with words so journalism seemed to be made for me, but I wasn't comfortable intruding into a person's private life. I kept clicking while the prostitute finished taking her clothes off and started taking off the lord's, but I had already vowed to myself that I'd never do it again.

Watching the pair have sex wasn't at all enjoyable. It made my skin crawl. The man was so far in his cups and the woman less than engaged with what she was doing that it was like watching a human jigsaw being put together. It was that impersonal. Didn't last long either—the lord definitely didn't get his money's worth.

As soon as they departed so did I. I developed the film. The photos came out well and my stomach churned when I looked at each one. Not just because the images were seedy and in some cases explicit but because my morals were being challenged. Mum had brought me up to respect people. We'd gone to church for years, until I'd hit my late teens and I'd decided I was too cool for Sunday school. In all those years I had been taught about compassion and love, and snooping on a man who was clearly in a very dark place didn't gel with that.

I thought about destroying the photos, but sadly I decided that I didn't want to face Lydia's wrath if I did. I had a work ethic too and my boss had asked me to complete a task. In the end that command won over everything else.

"These are amazing, India, absolutely fucking amazing." Lydia bounced up and down in her office chair, so much so I was afraid she was going to be shot into the air. "All the papers will want them. This will make you rich, my girl. This will kick-start your career."

She was right. My photos were in great demand there on in. Unfortunately it wasn't because of their quality or their artistic beauty. They wanted me to catch people in the act, whatever that act might be. I followed politicians to hotel rooms, I took photos of dirty money changing hands, vicars in casinos and judges snorting cocaine.

I felt sleazy doing it but my reason for doing it was pure, or so I thought. I was just establishing my name, making some money so that eventually I could drop the tabloid stuff and concentrate on serious news stories and taking photos of great merit. My dream was to take an iconic photo that would be used down the years to show future generations an act or an event that changed history.

Chapter Two

2003
Xander Patrick

"Mr. Patrick, Mr. Patrick!" someone with a high-pitched and wearingly familiar voice called my name.

I tried my best to ignore it but when a hand tapped me on my back I had to stop.

"Oh, sir. I've been calling you." Mary panted, hand on her chest. "I've chased after you from the shop."

"Sorry, Mary, I was thinking about Harriet."

"She's fine, sir, no signs yet, but I need to let you know something."

My eyeballs really wanted to roll but I fought hard to look interested. Mary always had to let me know something. Sometimes it was her lumbago, other times it was how terribly I was looking after my mother's business, and if I was really lucky she'd be trying to set me up on blind dates with her friend's daughters or granddaughters.

"What is it, Mary?" It wasn't difficult not to sound too interested.

"You know Gerald wrote in to that magazine—"

"*Readers' Wives*?"

"No." She shook her head, and I held in a smirk. "The one with the woman and the hair and the—"

"*Nuts*?"

"No, no, no. Not a food magazine. She writes the articles on the old houses and does the pictures. She's dead good."

"You mean *Good Manors*." I could have teased Mary further for my own entertainment but I really did have a busy day ahead.

"Yeah, that's the one. Well, she's coming."

"Oh, fabulous. Write the dates in the big diary." Stepping forward to pull away from the well-meaning but vastly annoying old woman, I was stopped by a hand on my arm.

"But, Xander, that's the thing." Her eyes were big and bright under the cloud of fluffy gray hair. "She's coming today!"

"Today?" I couldn't have a nosy journalist at Mallard's—the finances needed going over, there was a new arrival expected at any minute, and with a whole load of renovation in the offing the timing couldn't be worse.

"Yes, today."

"How in God's name can that be? No one told me. I wasn't informed."

"No, well, Gerald answered the phone yesterday and it was someone at the magazine asking if we could take India early, and he said yes and now she's coming today, expected about lunchtime, and I don't know what to do."

"Why the hell wasn't I asked about this?"

"You know Gerald, he's easily excitable and he thought it was a good thing. Her articles bring in the tourists."

"I know, but now? Why now? I haven't got time to be mollycoddling a bloody journalist!"

"You don't have to, that's the point. She joins in with the day-to-day running of the place. Where shall we put her?"

"Can't we just put her off? Get her to come back another time?"

Mary sucked air through the gap in the front of her teeth and shook her head.

"Gerald said we can't. The woman on the phone told him this was our only chance."

I ran my fingers through my hair in frustration. Whoever the woman on the phone was, she knew she'd been talking to an imbecile. A well-meaning imbecile with great knowledge of Mallard Hall and its history, but common sense were not well-used words in his dictionary.

"Right, fine then. I'll put her with bloody Gerald. He can deal with her. Let me know when she arrives, I need to meet with her."

"Okay, are you sure Gerald—?"

"He was so excited to have her here so he can deal with her," I snapped.

"Right, well, she can come in the shop with me tomorrow then, you know, so she gets a feel for the variety of the place."

"Sure, that's fine. Now let me get on, I need to see Harriet."

Sometimes I was convinced that only Harriet really listened to me, that only she understood me. Mallard's was my ultimate passion. To keep the hall open, to make it a success was all I dreamed about. It was difficult holding together that dream on my own but I battled on.

"Hello, sweetheart, how are you doing today?"

Harriet bleated and shuffled herself up onto her four legs and wobbled over to the gate as I let myself in.

"You're looking good, any sign of the little one?"

She bleated again, and I was sure I heard a weary note to the mother-to-be's voice.

"Oh, the little bundle of wool will be here soon enough, darling. Don't fret." I petted her. She was so soft and bouncy. That was why Castlemilk Moorit wool was so expensive and hence why I'd spent a small fortune on Harriet. She'd make her money back and more within a year from wool and maybe meat from her offspring. I was hoping to have a sizeable flock one day, but Harriet was my first and I was very protective of her.

"Well, my pet, I've got to get back to work. The books just don't seem to balance. God, Harriet. This place will be the death of me."

It had certainly killed my father. People said it was his bad boy ways, the drinking and the women and the gambling, but I knew the truth. Mallard Hall had consumed him. It wasn't easy to maintain a huge property and staff, especially when the family money had all but gone and you had no discernible business skill.

My dad had been brought up as aristocracy and had never learned a thing about business or a trade of his own. They had burned up money like it was fuel back through the fifties and sixties. It had only slowed down a little when my dad had married Mum and he'd inherited the hall. I'd looked at the books and it seemed he had been sensible for a while, trying to build up what little capital there had been.

It had all gone to pot in the eighties. I didn't really know all that had happened, Mum had never said, but everyone knew of Dad's reputation. He had been caught on camera once and that had become his complete demise. He had spiraled into debt and constant alcoholism. By the time I was twelve he was dead.

It had been a weird thing, almost a relief to know he was gone. I remembered in the back of my memory a cheerful man with a sparkling smile. He'd read me a bedtime story every night and had gone out of his way to be with me. Those memories were few and far between. I couldn't have been much older than five or six when he'd become distant, almost non-existent in fact. And when we had crossed paths he had simply yelled and hollered at me. He'd hit me, or when he'd been incredibly drunk he'd tried to hit me and had missed.

He hadn't been my dad, he had been the shell of him. So to have that shell gone was a relief, it meant I was able to cherish the good memories and attempt to forget the bad.

Mum had then taken over the reins at the Manor and she had started to whip it into shape, with a little help from me. We had been incredibly poor back then, personally speaking. Mum had pushed every last penny back in to the hall to keep it ticking over. I had been sixteen when I'd joined her more officially while doing a part-time course at college in accounting and business management. At eighteen I had become a full partner in the running of the hall, at twenty-one Mum had given me the hall as my birthday present, and that had been when I'd introduced the farm shop. She had supported me every step of the way, and even when she had been ravaged by the chemo that they'd tried to keep her alive with she had helped me out with whatever she'd been able to manage from her sickbed.

Every day I missed her. She had been my everything. Her life work had been Mallard Hall so I was determined to make it a success for her. It was the way I would keep her memory alive forever.

It was tough to make money in a country filled with stately homes. There had to be something different, something that pulled in the punters. The farm shop was working well for us, people from miles around came for our produce. Lamb, beef, chicken and not to mention the fruit and veg. We had connections with local farmers and cottage industries that brought in jams and preserves, cakes and biscuits and cheeses that bulked out our own produce. We were a hub for locally sourced food.

Several restaurants in the area used us to supply them, the rich 'holiday home in the country' set used us and the few distant tourists we attracted in came mostly for the farm shop and its award-winning produce. It was what dragged our revenue up and over the threshold. Or at least it had been. There'd been a worrying dip in the profits, and although stock seemed to be selling, the figures just weren't adding up.

My first thought had been petty thieving but Mary was a fantastic manager and her staff were by and large long-time, trusted employees. I'd put it down to the temps we brought in at busy times of the year but when I looked at the figures the money was draining at all times, not just in the school holidays and at Christmas.

It wasn't a paltry sum that had gone missing either. I might have been able to cast a blind eye if it had been. Times were tough and people had families to support. No, thousands of pounds a month had gone missing and it was seriously impacting the running of the whole manor.

I wandered into the shop.

"Mary, can I have a word?"

It was quiet—people came in on Thursdays, which was new stock day. Wednesday was quiet except for the odd bargain hunter or clueless tourist.

"Sure, sure, but you know we're expecting that India woman any moment. I'm going to go meet her because, well, I know you said to leave her with Gerald but we know what he's like. He'll bore the poor girl to tears in thirty seconds flat."

"Fine, fine, whatever. I've been going over the figures and it's not adding up, Mary. Are you sure that you're recording everything correctly?"

"Yes, Mr. Patrick. We take down all the stock here and check sales against it regularly. I've been checking the tills to make sure they aren't broken. I've been writing down every sale when I've been at 'em and then checking the takings. Always adds up perfectly." Mary looked worried. She knew what I was going to say next.

"Then we've got a thief, Mary. It's the only explanation."

She sighed and shook her fuzzy head. "But who, Xander? Who? I mean, most of the staff have all been here years. We've never had this problem before. They're all trustworthy sorts. I can't believe it of any of 'em."

"I know, Mary, but who else could it be? Are you checking up on people?"

"Yes, sir, I am. I'm doing random till checks and everything. I've not caught anyone stealing even a quid. There was the one time when Jenny was a fifty pence piece off but we found that on the floor, she must have dropped it. Spent ages looking for it. She was mortified, sir, didn't speak to me for a week after that."

"We need to do more, Mary. We're losing over ten percent of our takings. Who else has access to the tills?"

"No one really." Mary shrugged.

"Well, tell everyone to be extra vigilant. Watch customers, especially regulars, carefully."

"Oh, but, Mr. Patrick, we don't want to scare 'em off!"

Mary never quite knew what to call me. She'd known me since I'd been a kid but I was also her boss. I got a mix of titles when we talked.

"I know, Mary. But someone is on the take and if it's not staff it must be a customer. Make sure the tills are manned at all times. Make sure any unusual behavior is reported back to me."

"Right, okay, I will." Mary worried her hands together.

I hated doing that to her, she was a fantastic manager. When I had been little she'd been the housekeeper. She had kept all kinds of things in order, had kept me and my father apart when he had been particularly bad, where she'd been able to. When I had opened the shop I'd known she'd be perfect for it. She had been a bit reluctant at first, but when I had explained I was losing the role of housekeeper as the manor became more and more a tourist attraction she had agreed to give it a go. She had settled in well, apart from a few teething problems in the early days. She hadn't been keen on the tills at first but once she had gotten used to them she had been in her element. I was glad I'd managed to keep her on. She was ditzy and quite often terribly annoying but she could organize a bunch of prisoners into fine dining wait staff if she had to. The woman didn't know how to fail.

"I'm going back to the books. We've got several big bills to pay and I've got to work out how we can do it."

"I'll call you when India gets here then, shall I?"

"What? Who? Oh, her. Yes, yes, I suppose you should. Can you make sure she doesn't hear about our little problem then, please, Mary?"

"I will make sure of it, Xander. Mum's the word and all that." She placed a plump digit over her lips and winked at me. "I won't let another reporter ruin our lives. No way, I won't." Her face tightened into hard lines.

"Thanks, Mary."

All the old staff were of the same feeling. They knew of the article that had been printed at the height of my dad's alcoholism that seemed to be the catalyst of his demise. When I looked at the books for back then, there had been many gaps in the finances. Payments for prostitutes and single malt whisky, which he had never written down. *He just took, took, took.*

My mum had never let me see the article, wouldn't even talk about it with me.

"Your dad was a good man, Xander." Mum had sighed. "I want you to remember that. I don't want you to look at that tat."

"If he was so good, why did you change your name?" I had raged at her once, in a haze of teenage hormones and angst.

"Because I needed to step up and take over. Mallard's name is associated with dodgy deals, underhanded and sleazy goings-on. I needed to distance us from that to make this place work."

I hadn't got it at the time and I had kept the second name Mallard. It had only been when Mum had died that I had taken on her maiden name, a constant reminder of the woman who had loved me and had struggled on her own to rebuild a broken empire.

Mallard Hall was my pride and joy but Patrick was my family name. My dad was just a shadow but my mother lived on through me.

Chapter Three

India Grace

Packing for a *Good Manors* trip was always difficult. Overpacking was essential because sometimes I'd spend my days up to my boot tops in mud and other times I'd be attending balls and fundraisers and need my best dress and makeup. I had no clue what to expect at Mallard Hall and that was made worse by the sinking feeling in the pit of my stomach that I could get there to be chased away with pitchforks or a gun.

What if someone there remembered me and the photographs I'd taken? The guy who ran the show wasn't a Mallard, but what if his staff were old faithfuls from back in the day? I'd be screwed.

What did one wear when being pursued by angry, weapon-wielding folk anyway? I decided to pack nothing but sensible flat shoes just in case. Not that I was particularly known for sensible. I had extra-long hair that I frequently colored. At the time it was mostly my natural bronzed brown but the tips were dipped in pink, just the bottom couple of inches. I liked to be different, to dare and stand out. Funnily enough it was the easiest way to hide. Generally people were too afraid to approach someone with wacky hair and bright clothes, so I managed to slip through life quietly without much fuss and fluster.

Until I turned up to do a *Good Manors* shoot. I could tell how desperate the hall or manor I visited was by how enthusiastically I was greeted. If all was well, business booming, I'd be greeted quietly and efficiently. I loved those jobs because they were the easy ones. I got to take millions of photos and pick and choose what to use. The deeper the financial difficulty, the bigger the welcoming party.

When I pulled in at Mallard's, I knew they were in trouble and my stomach churned with the age-old guilt. Outside the grand Georgian frontage stood an old, gray-haired woman with glasses and a huge smile, a middle-aged guy with thinning hair, thick glasses and the body of a well-used broom and a young man with a confused look beneath his long fringe. It seemed to be a style he was comfortable with. As my car pulled up, the youngest of the three amigos ran off.

"India? India Grace?" The old woman's voice squeezed in through my partially open car window and attacked my ears.

I nodded.

"Fabulous!" She got even louder when I opened the door of the car and walked round toward the motley crew.

"Welcome to Mallard Hall, my dear. I'm Mary." She took my hand and viciously pumped it up and down in her own.

I was relatively sure she wasn't trying to wrench my arm out of my socket to bludgeon me with the wet end because she smiled at me the whole time. But maybe she was just crazy.

"Let me introduce you to Gerald. You already spoke on the phone."

"Hello, Gerald." I smiled, and he smiled back, revealing around five intact teeth and halitosis.

"Hello, love," he cried. "It's so good to see you here, to show Mallard's off to the world. It's a grand place, you know. Was built in 1764 by the original Lord Mallard. Look at the cornicing, it's a wonder it is."

"Yes, it's very lovely." I nodded. Clearly he was the historian of the group. There was always one, a mind filled with all the little facts, rumors and tales from the olden days. They had their uses—if I could stop them waffling on long enough to get them to answer my specific questions.

"See how symmetrical the place is? It goes all the way through the manor, you know."

I looked at the building with its tall, thin windows and its aching squareness. It was as symmetrical as could be, in comparison to the lush trees in the background growing willy-nilly like nature intended.

"Ah, here's Harry now with the master."

Mary skillfully butted in and stopped Gerald before he could spew any more random facts at me.

Coming round from the side of the building, the young, floppy-haired confused boy was being followed by a tall man in a sharp suit. His black hair curled slightly and bounced with every purposeful step.

"India Grace, I presume?" He stuck out his hand.

"Yes, from *Good Manors* magazine," I replied and reached forward, gripping his fingers in my own.

"Ah, good. I'm Xander Patrick, owner of Mallard Hall."

"Nice to meet you, Xander."

His grip was firm and businesslike, his gaze similar. Not a hint of warmth in the blue eyes that glared back at me. He wasn't very happy to see me. My heart trembled. Had he found out who I was? Did he know I had been the architect of the manor's downfall?

"Well, you've met the gang. They'll look after you. I'm rather busy right now but I'm sure I'll see you round."

I wanted to ask questions but before I could open my mouth again he'd let go of my hand and walked away. His elegant figure soon disappeared from sight.

"Don't mind Mr. Patrick," Mary chuckled. "He's a bit distracted at the moment. Harriet could give birth any second now."

Well, that explained it. He was married with a heavily pregnant wife. No wonder he didn't want me around the place. Shame he was taken, there was something very aesthetically pleasing about Xander Patrick.

"Right, well, if you follow me I'll take you up to your room, give you time to settle in. I'll come and get you in an hour or so then Gerald can give you a tour."

I nodded along, not really listening to her babbling. The young lad, Harry I think he was called, grabbed my luggage and followed us in. Of course we went in around the side—only the tourists used the front doors anymore, so Mary told me. That was pretty standard for most of the public halls I visited.

I didn't have time to take in any detail as Mary rushed me down a corridor and upstairs to the small room that was to be mine for the duration of the stay.

"It's not much, but all the posh renovated rooms are for the visitors to see. I hope you don't mind that you're in a poky servants' room—most of us are."

"You live here then, Mary?"

"Oh yes, two rooms down the corridor, in fact. Now, is everything okay for you?"

"Yes, it'll be fine." I smiled reassuringly.

"Good, good. I'll leave you be. I'll send young Harry up for you in an hour or so. Give you time to unpack and unwind before you get started."

"Thank you."

Mary bobbed and glided out of the room then closed the heavy wooden door behind her.

The room was spartan but clean and practical. I sat on the bed and it seemed pleasantly firm and not too squeaky. The walls were plain white, the curtains chintzy floral to match the bedcover and that really was that for detail. I popped my clothes in the dark wood wardrobe and chest of drawers that dominated one side of the small room then checked out the door adjacent to me.

The en suite bathroom was small and perfectly functional. Clearly it was relatively new, just popped into the next room along because it was the same size as the bedroom itself. I knew I'd be perfectly comfortable for the few nights I'd be there.

Some manors would set me up in a grand guest bedroom but they intimidated me. I didn't feel like it was the kind of room I belonged in. I was always much happier in a more modest setting. I took some time to check over my camera and set up my laptop. I had to keep focused on my job. If I let my mind slip for even a moment I would spiral down into self-defeating depression again and I promised myself I wouldn't let that happen.

The news of Lord Mallard's death had hit me really hard. I'd quit journalism and hidden away from the world for months afterward. I'd locked myself away in my flat and wished for death—had set out to take it one day in fact. A life for a life—at the time it had seemed fair. I'd be forever grateful to the person who'd pulled me out of that flunk. I'd tell them every day if I could but it had been a random incident with a stranger I'd never seen again that had changed the tide. I'd often mused that maybe she was an angel.

The knock on the door startled me into action.

"Miss, you're wanted in the main hall by Gerald. He's going to take you on the tour." Harry's tone of voice didn't lift or fall. I wondered if he ever expressed emotion.

"Oh, great. Let me grab my camera bag and notepad." I picked up my things and followed the young man downstairs.

"Have you worked here long?" I asked as Harry walked in front of me back the way I'd come with Mary earlier. I was glad he was with me. I was notoriously terrible with directions and had gotten lost in a fair few stately manors in the past.

"Not long, miss, no. Mr. Patrick hired me and a couple of other lads earlier in't year. I've done casual work for him on and off since being a kid so I jumped at the chance of working here proper like now I'm grown up." That was the longest sentence Harry had strung together since I'd arrived and he'd even managed to appear somewhat animated.

"Grown up?" I laughed.

"I'm eighteen now, miss, I've got to look after myself. I can do that working for Mr. Patrick." He looked contented, well, the bit of him I could see under his hair.

"Are you enjoying it here?"

"Oh, it's not bad, miss, not bad. Always something different going on."

He waited for me at the bottom of the stairs and even smiled. It was awkward to tell but I was pretty certain it was a smile and not just wind. He'd be a fairly good-looking guy one day, when he grew into his limbs and decided to cut his hair.

"Thanks, Harry." Gerald nodded at me and waved the young man away. "You can get back to the shop now." From the look on Gerald's face, he wasn't too keen on the younger lad.

"Ah, Miss Grace, I hope your room is sufficient for you." His grin was disconcerting. Half of it was missing.

"Yes, more than ample. And you can call me India."

He nodded and continued talking. "Now, we decided it would be a good idea to give you a tour of the place first so you can get a bit of an overview. Then tomorrow you can spend time in different parts of the estate and look at them more in depth."

"Sounds good to me." I found it useful to get the lay of the land early on, then I could work out exactly where to concentrate my future efforts, so I could find the interesting characters and the real stories behind the posh façade. That was what people read the article for, that was what I always felt pressured to find, and it wasn't always easy.

Gerald was a mine of information, most of it completely useless or tidbits I already knew. I nodded a bit and took the odd photograph as we toured the public parts of the building. It was a beautiful hall, lovingly renovated. I was impressed by how much had been put into it. The attention to detail was staggering.

"We're looking to adding new rooms over the next few years, the library and the old working kitchen, if we can raise the funds, of course. It costs a pretty penny to run all this. Hence why we've got the new-fangled shop. It's supposed to make money."

"Is it?" I asked, innocently. Or at least I aimed for innocently.

"Oh, yeah. Sort of, I suppose. More of a waste of time in my opinion, but then Mr. Patrick does like his little projects." Gerald chuckled and led me out of the grand house into the gardens.

"We'll go over and take a look now, Miss Grace, then I'll take you over to see the master's very latest project. He'd be well made up if they featured in your article."

I just nodded and followed Gerald across the graveled courtyard to a building that looked later than the original building, probably a stable added on a century or so after the original place was built. Or maybe the old equivalent of a granny flat or even a house for a mistress of an ancient Mallard.

I shook my head and took a deep breath. I didn't want to think about old Mallards. That was too painful. I focused on how well the place seemed to be doing, wanting to bury the guilt of decades past. It was a shame the old place had passed out of the family's hands but at least it was being preserved. I didn't want to think about what had happened to the rest of the Mallard family.

Getting closer to the red brick building, I noticed the modern double-glazed doors and started to see the modifications that had been made to the original exterior.

Inside it could have passed for a posh supermarket, with shelving and refrigerated cabinets. It was a very homey and welcoming environment, helped by Mary's ever smiling face.

"Hello again, miss. I hope Gerald's taking good care of you."

I nodded with fake enthusiasm, just to be polite.

"This is my pride and joy, built from nothing. Everything in here is sourced from the local community—a good chunk of it comes from the estate itself. Most of the meat on this counter is from the various livestock on our farm." Mary puffed her ample chest out with pride.

"Yes, yes, well, Miss Grace will be here with you tomorrow so you don't need to tell her everything now," Gerald snapped sulkily.

Mary rolled her eyes then shook her head. "Right, fine, Gerald. I guess you're rushing off somewhere important."

"Yes, we are," he snapped again. "Come along, Miss Grace."

Gerald turned to head back out of the door, and Mary leaned over the counter and whispered, "Gerald hates any modern additions. I'll show you the good stuff tomorrow."

It was clear that there were some interesting characters to get to know at Mallard Hall. That would make my article easier to write.

"Okay, now we'll go out to the farm and check out the other one of Mr. Patrick's crazy new projects."

The green surroundings kept my interest when we walked because Gerald was talking but I wasn't listening. Something about the original landscaping and the architect, all boring twaddle that was definitely not story worthy. I realized I would have to write the article of my lifetime to do this place justice and compensate for the hurt I'd done. I knew I'd never be able to make up fully for the mistakes of my youth but I had to try. Amending for those mistakes consumed my every action.

"So before we go in, miss, we need to wash our hands. So we don't pass anything on to the sheep and vice versa."

I snapped back to paying attention to Gerald and followed his lead, washing my hands then drying them on my jeans.

"Now we need to be quiet, miss. Harriet's in here and she's a bit jumpy."

"Harriet?" I mused. "Does she work on the farm as well then?" I remembered Xander mentioning something about Harriet being pregnant. It seemed weird that a pregnant woman would be allowed to work with livestock, especially if she was so close to dropping the sprog.

"Well, I guess you could say that. She's meant to be anyway. She's the master's latest hare-brained plan." Gerald sighed. It seemed like a very rude way to reference the master's wife.

"Are they only recently married then?"

"Married?" Gerald looked over his shoulder at me as we walked into the darkened, cool interior of the barn. "Mr. Patrick is devoted to Harriet but they're not married, good Lord no." He laughed.

Well, that put me in my place. I supposed a man in this day and age didn't need to be married to a woman to be having a kid with her.

"But surely a heavily pregnant woman shouldn't be out here in a barn. Not unless she's giving birth to some kind of messiah anyway." I laughed at my poor joke, but Gerald just looked confused.

"Woman? What woman? Harriet is a Castlemilk Moorit."

"What's that? Sounds rude to me."

"A sheep, Miss Grace. Harriet is a sheep."

Looking over the metal barrier, sure enough there was a sheep. Shaggy fleeced and horned. Harriet didn't look too impressed at all.

"Oh, I see."

"Why, what did you think she was?"

"Mr. Patrick's wife."

Gerald's shoulders shook, his mouth curled up into a bow, and he bent forward to slap his knee. All without making a sound. When the laugh came it began with a concerning wheeze and ended in a whooping cough. No wonder Gerald didn't look like he laughed much—it sounded like if he did too much of it it'd kill him.

"No, the master's single. Not had a woman here since his mother passed this six months since, and there weren't many before that to be truthful."

"I got the wrong end of the stick then."

"Aye, you did, miss. This is Harriet, she's expected to birth any day now, hence Mr. Patrick's anxious demeanor. He paid a pretty penny for her. She's a rare breed and he wants to make a flock. Sell the fleeces to make cash. To use 'em as a draw. He wants to have loads of different rare breeds in the end, but at the moment it's just Harriet here."

"She seems like a very lovely animal," I responded. Sheep weren't a specialism of mine, even though I'd done a couple of years at veterinary college before I'd followed my heart into journalism. Harriet did look healthy to me even if I didn't know the specifics of her breed. She made a snuffling, lowing sound, so Harriet appreciated my complimentary words.

"Aye, I suppose she is. Complete folly like, but that ain't her fault."

"Seems like a sound business plan to me. People are all about the rare breeds and local sourcing these days." I wasn't sure I liked Gerald's moaning tone. Anything new seemed to be dismissed by him, like he wanted to live in the past.

"Just what I keep telling him, Miss Grace, but Gerald is stuck in his ways."

I jumped and looked round. Xander Patrick's frame filled the doorway.

Gerald didn't even have the good grace to look flustered.

"She's not looking any closer to birthing, Mr. Patrick. Do you think we need to get the vet up?"

Xander pulled air between his teeth and rolled up his short sleeves.

"I don't know, Gerald, but I'm inclined to let nature take its course a bit longer. She's not in any distress." He kicked himself over the barrier with little effort then moved across the straw toward the expectant mother, who seemed not to be at all worried about the invasion of her space.

"Hello, sweetheart," he murmured lovingly. "How are you doing?"

Xander had been quite cold and aloof when we'd first met. I saw a completely new side to him as he tenderly stroked the fleece of his pride and joy.

"She's a beautiful animal," I commented. The atmosphere felt a little heavy, like I'd walked in on an intimate moment that I wasn't part of.

"She's an absolute peach. There's only a few flocks of the Castlemilks in the world, you know. Harriet is one of the rarest sheep in the UK at the moment."

"Wow, really?" I hadn't realized how valuable she was. After all, she was a sheep—those I'd had dealings with had never been worth a particularly large amount of money.

"Yep. When I was looking into a sheep to buy I thought I might as well start with the rarest." Xander's face lit up, like he was talking about a child. "She's going to be the savior of this place."

Gerald coughed heavily, and considering I'd not heard him cough before I was certain it was a tactical sound, not an actual malaise.

"Well, her and the shop and the tours. We're not that badly off." Xander shrugged, his cheeks reddening.

I wondered if they'd turn the same shade when he was fucking and blinked a couple of times to get that image out of my head.

"Well, it's not news that Mallard Hall has been struggling to survive and I know it's not easy to bring a stately home back from the brink. I think you're doing all the right things, though. I'm no expert but I've seen my fair share of failing country houses and this one doesn't feel like it's failing."

Gerald mumbled something, but Xander smiled widely at me.

"Thank you, it's really good to hear a stranger say that. I keep telling myself it's getting better, but, well, it's been a struggle."

I swear I saw tears in his eyes but he looked back to Harriet, and Gerald intervened. "Right, miss, I think that's that for the tour. We'll be getting together for dinner at seven, will you join us?"

"Sure." I nodded and followed him out of the barn. "Bye," I shouted back in the general direction of Xander, but he didn't respond. What a strange man he was.

Chapter Four

Xander Patrick

'I'm no expert but I've seen my fair share of failing country houses and this one doesn't feel like it's failing.'

I'd felt my eyes welling as I'd thanked India for her words. I'd been working far too hard for such a little thing to set me off. Grief was a weird beast, rearing its head at the strangest moments.

Mum had striven to bring the hall back from ruin—it seemed so cruel that the cancer had gotten to her before she'd seen the fruits of all her determined attention. Mum was better than the way her life ended. Every ounce of vitality had drained from her. In the last weeks she had been merely a body—all personality and soul had left her already.

I'd dropped everything to care for her in those end days, that had been tough, but as much of a negative impact it had had on the hall's recovery, I wouldn't change that for anything. Mum had been my rock all through my life. My mum was my childhood.

An only child with a silly stutter and acute shyness, I hadn't done well with my peers. My mum had been a teacher before she'd met and married my dad so she'd homeschooled me from when I was six years old. Some would say that I missed out on a proper education but my top-level qualifications would tell you otherwise.

Dad's death had been a shock, but I couldn't say I really grieved for him. I had been more concerned about my mum, and all I'd cared about was her happiness and wellbeing.

Mum hadn't looked twice at another man from that day on, though many had tried to court her. She had been focused solely on the hall and bringing it back from the brink.

"If these fellas think I have two thrupenny bits to rub together they're mistaken," she used to say. "I'm poorer than a church mouse and the roof over my head's got a great big hole in it."

She had never really complained, just got on with it. She had raised funds and livestock, she had built up visits and walls and had even had a go at the electrics a time or two. She had been fearless and happy to get on overalls and get dirty. I got my hands-on approach from her—nothing was too lowly for me to do.

I missed her every day. Her wit, her smile, her warmth. She'd been able to wrap anyone around her little finger and get what she wanted. I hadn't inherited that trait from her at all. I wasn't a people person, I definitely preferred sheep. Every day was a struggle. I had to motivate the staff, balance the books and keep everything running smoothly. And so many things had clogged up the works of late that India's words had come as a balm out of the blue.

And I cried. I'd barely spoken to her and she'd seen me cry. I knew she'd noticed. She was sharp-eyed.

Those eyes, they were a wonderful shade of green too. Big and bright and I could read a world of intelligence in them. She'd seen my tears and I didn't know what to do about that. So I just focused in on Harriet.

And therein lay another worry. If she was breech or there was some other complication with the birth I wasn't sure I could afford the vet bill, but if I lost the lamb, or God forbid, Harriet too, we'd be right in the shit. It seems ridiculous to say the fate of the hall was in the fleece of one sheep but it was true.

Everything else seemed to be losing money. The shop, which had been a fabulous earner, had taken a fall in profits, and the tours never made enough money to cover their staffing and the upkeep of the public areas of the hall.

So the only hope was Harriet and the start of my rare breed farm, my dream. The dream that would not only save Mallard's but make it stand out from the others. In a country packed with historic buildings, I knew I had to do something special with mine.

Harriet wasn't looking any closer to being a mother than she had been when I'd last checked her. I patted her side and left the pen.

"I'll be back later, girl." I talked easily to Harriet—she was the only woman in my life who understood me and she wasn't even the same species as me.

Summed up my luck, really. Of course I'd had a few girlfriends over the years, sort of loved a few of them, but not one had stuck with me for more than a few months. Some had been gold-diggers, others simply hadn't been able to handle how much time I spent with Mum, and since she had passed away I'd not even had a promise of a date.

The sun was setting when I headed back toward the main house. I planned to grab a sandwich or something to eat while I worked some more on the finances. Mary always invited me into the kitchen to eat with the staff who stayed in, but I never felt very comfortable eating with them.

Not that Mary, Gerald, Harry and Jenny had ever been anything less than welcoming, but I always felt like I was imposing. That they'd be able to relax a lot easier if I wasn't there. I isolated myself I suppose, but I'd never been afraid of my own company. *Although I wouldn't mind keeping India company for a while.*

She was cute, no denying that, and she seemed quite pleasant, for a journalist.

'Never trust them, son, never trust that they'll tell your story or that they'll not twist your words out of all proportion. Journalists thrive on bringing people like us down.'

Mum's words echoed in my head. Clearly anyone connected to newspapers had been scum in her books. Dad wasn't perfect, and Mum had been the first to say their relationship hadn't been brilliant, but his death had hurt her and she'd been convinced he'd never have killed himself if those horrible exposé photos of him hadn't made it into the press.

But surely she hadn't meant people like India. She wrote for a respectable magazine. I didn't have much time for pleasurable reading but I had caught a couple of India's articles. We always had a copy or two of *Good Manors* available for guests to flick through. A good word from India could double footfall, I'd heard. I'd never read anything but a pleasant review from her. She was very careful in her use of language and any problems would be there if you read between the lines but on the face of it she was always polite.

We could really do with the India factor, it was just bad timing. A year or so down the line when the flock was established and I'd worked out where the hole in my finances was and plugged it, then India's visit would be a godsend. As it was, she'd come at a pivotal moment where everything was held in the balance and even her presence could tip the scales in the wrong direction.

If everything went terribly wrong, how could even India Grace put a positive spin on it? Mallard Hall would be ruined. If India had turned up at a different time maybe I'd have been tempted to try out my rusty seduction technique on her. I couldn't allow her to distract me at such a crucial point, though. I really wanted to hold her close to me and taste her lips and do other darker, baser things to her, but I couldn't. I had to keep things purely professional or my business would end up down the pan.

I wasn't paying much attention to where I was walking. I never really did, it was like my shoes knew their way around the place without my brain having to give directions. So when I came body to body with a blockage I was quite easily tipped back onto my arse. And as an instinctual reaction I grabbed onto the item that had destabilized me and pulled it down on top of me.

"Oh my God, Xander, I mean, Mr. Patrick, oh shit, are you all right?"

"Yes, I'm fine, are you okay?"

India's warm curves pressed me down into the soft grass. I tried not to think too much about her body so I wouldn't embarrass myself.

"Oh, yeah, yeah, nothing broken." Her gaze kept me pinned down. Her cheeks were flushed and her hair draped forward and into my face, the pink tips tickling my nose.

I wiped it away and hooked it around the back of her ear without thinking.

"Jeez, I should get up off you, shouldn't I?" She shook her head and scrambled backward.

I watched her breasts swaying in the bright turquoise top and coughed. I hoped she hadn't caught me leering at her. I couldn't help it, she fascinated me.

"Sorry, again." She scrambled to her feet and smoothed down her long, white skirt. "Do you need a hand up?" Thrusting her hand forward, she smiled down at me.

I reached up and took the proffered fingers in mine. I attempted not to put too much of my weight on her as I scrambled up. Her fingers were smooth and delicate, her hand cool in my own. I didn't want to let go.

"Thanks." I grinned. "I think I should be the one apologizing. I wasn't paying any attention to where I was going, I was walking on autopilot."

"Oh, no, no. I didn't see you coming either. I was wrapped up in thinking about stuff to add into my article."

"All good, I hope." I was still holding her hand and was sure she was as aware of it as I was. I didn't know how to let it go. I mean, clearly I knew physically what to do, but I was caught in the awkwardness of the situation. I didn't want to be the one to let go first, I didn't want her to think I was eager to get away. An awkward schoolboy had nothing on me. Hot cheeks, tapping foot, dried mouth. I might not be the heart and soul of a party but usually I was cool, calm, collected and able to hold a whole conversation with someone without dithering. Not with India, though.

"It's a secret." She winked. Squeezed my hand and let it drop. "I don't tell anyone before it comes out in the magazine."

Oh God, she thinks I'm an idiot.

I cringed internally. Clearly all the weird chemistry stuff was on my side only. I'd have to restrain myself.

"Sure, of course, well, I better go. I've got so much to do."

I didn't wait to hear what else she had to say. I walked off, but I might as well have run away crying. It was so obvious I was making a tactical retreat. I didn't have time or energy to waste on being infatuated with a woman. Especially a journalist. Mum had often tried to match-make me with suitable women. She'd not even have put India down on a reserves list. I resigned myself to a life of singledom, dead on track to becoming a crazy sheep man.

Chapter Five

India Grace

I felt like I'd offended Xander with my lie. I mean, it was partly true, I never told a soul what would go into my article, not even the boss, before I'd got it down on paper.

Maybe he'd thought I'd been rude or that I was a bit weird. Ridiculously, it disturbed me that maybe he didn't like me. I hardly knew him. But maybe he'd change his mind in the future. Turning things to the positive had never been my strong suit but after some particularly effective therapy I'd started to do it more often, or at least attempted to.

On a whim I decided to head up to see Harriet. She'd liked me and she was behind bars, so I wouldn't be able to fall on her. Dusk had fallen, the grounds' bright foliage was muted with the heated glow of the setting sun giving the ambience of an old-fashioned photo, blurred around the edges and a little faded.

I was surprised by how much I enjoyed being around livestock again. Harriet reminded me of my days in veterinary school, but more importantly she reminded me of my work experience and the man who'd overseen it.

When I'd first gone to university I had started out studying to be a vet. Mum had wanted me to be a doctor but I didn't want that, so vet had been the compromise. I had gotten a couple of years in before I'd grown a pair and put my foot down. I hadn't wanted to struggle in a job for the rest of my life. I'd wanted to have a career that linked in with my passions – English and art.

Mum hadn't been impressed but I had been much happier. Some of the vet stuff had stuck, though. Especially as I'd had a couple of work-experience places where I'd got to be a bit hands-on. One of the placements had been with a rural vet in the spring. I'd seen a lot of livestock born that year, I'd even assisted in a few of the births myself.

Actually, the vet I had been with was a very good-looking older man called Tom. I'd struggled at times to keep my mind on the job. He had such long, nimble fingers, I would get distracted thinking about how they'd feel on different parts of my body. Even knowing where he sometimes stuck said hands hadn't put me off.

It had been the last day of my placement when I had acted on my lusts. We'd been in the local for a bevy after my last shift with him. He'd had the rest of the day off and I had been waiting for a train home. The trains came along once every blue moon, but I hadn't minded spending a bit more time with him.

It had been somewhere partway through my third glass of wine – on an all but empty stomach – that I'd told him how fascinated I was by his hands.

"Really?" he'd said, putting down his pint, then turning them left and right. "These old things?"

I had nodded eagerly and he'd stretched out to take my hand in his.

"I think your fingers are far more attractive, though. Soft and supple and so pretty."

I had virtually come in my jeans right then and there. For the duration of my visit, I'd been imaging how his hands would feel and I was about to find out.

"Thank you." I had giggled as he'd turned and stroked my hands with his.

"Well, I think all of you is very attractive, to be truthful. I've wanted to tell you that since the day you arrived but it didn't seem professional to do so."

"Well, I'm no longer training with you," I had whispered and looked up into his big, brown eyes. They had usually been so mild, so calming, but at that moment they had been streaked with lightning bolts of gold and my stomach had clenched at the thought of what that might have meant.

"Not to be a vet, no," he had said with a wink. "But if you'd like to come back to my place with me, I think I have the perfect position for you."

I wasn't very good at directions at the best of times, and as I was distracted by a trip down memory lane I soon ended up a bit lost. Of course the farm contained many buildings, not just the one housing the mother-to-be I wanted to visit, and to me they all looked alike. I heard giggling in one, a high and a low voice joined in harmony. I was relieved—someone was there to help direct me. I dipped around the side of the building, looking for the entrance. It was worn and cracked, straw-yellow peeking through the rough brown of years-old creosote.

I should have realized it was a bit quiet and wondered what the people were doing in the barn so late on in the evening but I simply strolled in without thinking. It became apparent on entering that once upon a time the place had been stables capable of housing at least a half dozen horses.

Taking in my dim surroundings, I didn't call out. I wasn't convinced I'd really heard anyone in there after all and didn't want to shout out to people who probably weren't even there. I felt stupid enough already. A soft bump followed by a guttural moan startled me. That moan rose to a sigh over the shuffling of feet.

Fuck, that's not a working sound.

I froze, not sure what to do next. Had they heard me come in? The stable in front of me had a fallen slat. I couldn't quite see what was going on as it was dim within the wooden walls but I was sure I saw movement. My natural, journalistic instinct kicked in and I slowly moved forward, paying great attention to where I was stepping whilst still trying to peer through the gap. Anyone who walked in would have thought I was a short-sighted granny who'd lost her walking stick the way I hobbled.

I bent forward and peeked through. I wasn't prepared for the vision that greeted me. It wasn't surprising to see Harry and Jenny fooling around—it had been very obvious that those two were infatuated with each other—but I didn't expect to see Jenny tied to the bars that divided this stable from the next with what looked like very old and very itchy rope.

"This is what you get for making goo-goo eyes at that journalist woman," Harry growled, licking his lips and flexing a leather belt in his hands. He looked good without his shirt on. He had muscles underneath all that dark and broody slouching.

"But I wasn't—"

She was cut off by the crack of leather against her wobbling buttocks. I bit my lip to hold in a gasp.

"What have I told you about talking back, Jenny?"

"Sorry, Sir." She gasped.

"Well, you will be, my love."

I couldn't process what I was hearing and seeing. Jenny had been quiet, had barely said a word to me, and here was young Harry laying into her because she fancied me. She didn't, did she? I hadn't picked up on any lustful vibes, at least not directed at me.

For a moment I thought about speaking up, stepping in and stopping it all, but then I noticed that Jenny's responses to the lash of the leather were loud but she was enjoying it. The yelps and curses were interjected with moans and gasps of pure arousal.

I flashed back quickly to my time with Tom, the same sound, the same moans, but coming from my lips as he'd belted me for something he'd also made up.

"You would, though."

Harry's voice pulled me back to reality.

"You'd fuck her if you could." He was stood directly behind her, running his hand over her buttocks.

"Yes," she gasped breathily, "yes I would."

She didn't do anything for me, yet that choked confession pooled right between my thighs. I should have left them in peace but I couldn't resist continuing to peek. My pulse was beating all through my body, my head, my heart, my pussy.

Harry dipped his fingers between Jenny's ample, pinked buttocks and pressed them inside her.

"Fuck, that's hot," he growled against her ear then pulled her ponytail. "But you're mine, remember that, Jen."

"Yes, Sir."

"Good girl."

Harry let his trousers down, revealing a thick erection for a matter of moments before he shuffled forward and filled his girlfriend with it. Reality hit as I watched them passionately copulate. When they finished, what would they do if they found me?

I quietly hurried out of the old stables, heart thumping and mind swimming with erotic images. My blood buzzed as I crept through the darkened farmyard, wondering where the hell I was. My feet on the grass and gravel sounded loud, interspersed with creaks of wood and cheeps and scrambles of nature. The rumble of contented livestock and the distant call of an owl enveloped me. I walked from one dreamlike scene to another. I tried hard not to panic. If all else failed I had my phone and I could ring the house for help. I didn't want to, but if I had to I could.

The glow of an exposed bulb round a familiar barn door filled me with joy—by sheer coincidence I'd found Harriet.

I'd found Xander too. I immediately realized something wasn't right. Harriet lay in the hay, as you'd expect for a mother nearing birth, but Xander looked pained and anxious seated in the hay beside her.

"Hey," I greeted. "How's it going?"

"Not good." He shook his head. "She's been straining for over an hour and there's nothing yet."

"Has she expelled the water bag?" My old training kicked in and I started to analyze what might be wrong.

"Yes." He nodded and ran his fingers through his hair. "I think I need to call the vet."

"Have you got gloves, hot water and soap?"

"Yes. Well, I can easily get them for you." He looked confused.

"I'll need lubricant too. Hurry and bring everything to me."

Xander didn't even question my request, just rushed off. Harriet moaned and shuddered.

"Hello, girl," I soothed, climbing into the stall with her. "It's all right, Harriet, I'm here. I'll give the little one a hand, don't worry." I patted her side, and she shuddered again. *Poor thing.* It was probably her first lamb, and young mums were more likely to have complications.

Xander brought me everything I needed and I got on with scrubbing myself clean and preparing to help this poor mother out.

"Do you know what you're doing?" he asked once I had my arm inside his very expensive sheep.

"Bit late to ask that now, but yes, I trained to be a vet for a while." I smiled over at him then cocked my head to the side. "Ah, there's the problem, little one's got its elbows locked and mum can't push it any farther down."

Scrunching up my face, I concentrated on manipulating the lamb backward a bit until the legs extended straight.

"Right." I pulled my hand free. "She should be able to do the rest herself."

"How did you know what to do?" Xander asked as Harriet once more shivered and shook with a contraction.

"Veterinary school, like I said. Mum wanted me to be a doctor, I couldn't stomach it so we compromised and I trained to be a vet. It wasn't my calling, though, and after two years I changed my degree to journalism and the rest is history."

"So you've done this before? I mean, practically." Xander carefully watched Harriet, petting her nose tenderly.

"No, I only ever read about it." I looked up from washing my arms in the soapy water and focused on looking solemn. His face dropped, and I laughed. "Of course I've done it before, spent time with a country vet in the spring. I brought many animals into the world, including a few sheep."

"Good, sorry, I'm a bit all over the place. Harriet means so much to me, to the hall, I didn't know what to do. I've read up, I talked to the vet, but I just froze." He sighed. The poor man was seriously frazzled.

"It's okay." I ran my hand down his arm. "It's difficult to know when to intervene and you can do more harm than good if you don't know what you're doing. Hey, look, the nose is appearing."

I'm sure the relief showed through my voice. I was confident that the birth was finally going the way it should.

"Oh yeah." Xander's face lit up. "Look at that!"

"Won't be long now. Look, already the legs are following through!"

"It's amazing," he gasped.

"A miracle," I sighed as the little life burst forth from the relieved ewe. She immediately set to looking after her offspring, licking its face to remove the mucus. Soon the little thing was bleating happily.

"Harriet's a brilliant mum." I smiled. "She's a natural."

Chapter Six

Xander Patrick

"God, India, thank you. I'd have lost her without you."

I'd been completely paralyzed with fright. I'd read up so much on what to expect from the labor and what might go wrong, but I couldn't seem to remember any of it as I'd watched Harriet strain and strain again.

She shrugged. "You'd have rung the vet if I hadn't shown, it was an easy fix. I'm sure it would all have been fine."

"Well, still, thank you."

She'd come in and just gotten on with it. Who'd have thought she had experience in lamb delivery? She sat down in the hay beside me with a flop and squeezed my arm.

"You're welcome. It was good to help and it's always a rush to see a cute baby animal."

The little brown ball of fluff tottered on its towering legs, and Harriet bleated encouragement.

"The little thing is adorable," I acknowledged.

"So what made you decide on rare breed sheep?"

"Oh, well, I wanted something a bit different but within the bounds of something we already had here on the estate. I made a list of loads of things then went through each one for its merits and down points, and rare breeds came out with the best differential."

"You went with your gut then." She chuckled.

"Yeah." I nodded. "I'm not very good at that. Let's just say stuff from my youth showed me the downside of being impulsive. Everything I do these days is calculated."

"Yeah, I understand." India sighed. "But my impulses still seem to get me into trouble."

"I owe you an apology, too. I've been standoffish since you got here. I'd calculated having you visit into my plans but I wasn't expecting you this week. Gerald took that decision into his own hands. It's thrown me off a bit but I shouldn't have taken it out on you."

"No worries." India's smile really was a sight to behold. Her green eyes sparkled and her whole face lit up with joy. "I don't think many people would welcome me dropping by at such short notice, and I didn't mean to be rude earlier, you just startled me, well, we startled each other, I suppose."

"No, I didn't mean to be rude either." I looked down at my toes, noticing just how scuffed and muddy my black shoes were. "Maybe we should start from scratch, yeah?"

"Good idea." India pushed her hand out in front of her. "Hello, I'm India Grace, reporter for *Good Manors* magazine."

I grasped her hand in mine. Her fingers were slightly chilly. I noticed for the first time that she wasn't wearing a coat.

"Hello, I'm Xander Patrick, the man in charge here. Nice to meet you, India, and welcome to Mallard Hall."

"Thank you."

We parted hands, and India shivered.

"Are you okay? Would you like my jacket?"

"No, no, I'll be fine. I should probably be getting back. I was only meant to be taking a brief walk. I've got to be up and in the shop in the morning."

"Let me walk you back to the hall, then. Harriet and the lamb are fine, aren't they?"

India nodded. "Looks it to me. Oh, has she passed the placenta yet?" She scoured the floor visually then stood up. "Yep, she has, we need to get rid of this. She'd probably eat it but you don't want it left around to encourage vermin."

Between us we cleaned up the afterbirth, checked the mum and child had all the supplies they needed, flicked off the light then walked away from the barn. I took a deep, satisfied breath. For the first time in weeks I didn't feel a tightness in my shoulders, a heaviness of heart. Maybe Harriet's successful lambing was the start of an upturn in my luck. I really hoped so.

India shuddered, and I took off my leather jacket. Old and battered, it was what I always wore when a suit wasn't dictated.

"Here"—I slipped it over her shoulders—"you'll freeze otherwise."

"Thanks." She pulled the edges together. "It has gone really cold tonight."

"They're predicting a frost, even though it's late in the season." I didn't know why I needed to pass on that nugget of information.

"I bet. Are you okay? You're not cold, are you?"

"No, my old sweater's keeping me warm enough, thank you." It seemed strange that she was worried about me. Women I'd been with in the past would have expected this kind of behavior—they had expected me to be a gentleman. But then, they'd all expected me to be rich too. When they'd found out I wasn't, they'd left.

"I'll come out with a jacket for my constitutional tomorrow night."

"Now that's an old-fashioned word." Her use of it struck me as my mum had enjoyed a constitutional every evening while she'd been able. It had only been the last few months of her life when we hadn't managed to get out for an evening stroll.

"I like it. My mum used to use it. Only when we were on holiday, though. I'm not sure anyone takes a constitutional around a housing estate." India smiled.

"My mum liked the word too." My voice faltered.

"Are you all right?" she asked.

"Yes." I sighed. "Just she passed away six months ago and it's still raw at times."

"Yeah, I understand. My mum died three years ago but there's still times when I miss her so much it physically hurts."

We walked on in silence. I was lost in remembrances of Mum and I wondered what she'd have made of India. She had had a dislike of journalists, but I was sure she couldn't have held that against such a sweet, thoughtful woman. Although, maybe she would have. She had always been very stubborn. She had also been very vocal about me never settling for anything less than perfect for me. Though her vision of perfect and mine often hadn't been the same.

"So you're in the shop tomorrow." I had to stop thinking and interact some more. I spent far too much of my time alone with my own thoughts.

"Yes, that's right. Mary's showing me the ropes."

"Good luck with that." I chuckled. "Mary's quite a character."

"Yeah, I'd noticed. She seems lovely, though."

"Oh yes, she is. She just never ever shuts up. I swear she gets her way more often than not simply because she talks at me so much I give in to make her stop."

"Oh, I know your Kryptonite now," she purred throatily.

"Damn, I shouldn't have let that out so easily." I shook my head dramatically.

"It's okay, I won't use it against you immediately. I'll get you warmed up a bit first."

"Said the vicar to the nun," I responded without thinking.

"Ha, more like the vet to the… Never mind, let's not go there."

The laughter we shared was genuine, and when we came to the hall I was a little saddened that our interaction was over.

"Thanks, Xander." She handed me my coat back.

"And thank you, India," I replied. "I'm glad you were here tonight."

"Yeah, me too."

For a moment I was sure she was going to push up and kiss me. I tipped my head down toward her, preparing to accept her lips on mine, but then she coughed and I coughed and we awkwardly shuffled apart.

"I'll see you tomorrow then?" she called.

"I'm sure you will. Bye."

And she disappeared upstairs. I walked up a little way behind her. My room was at the opposite end of the corridor, still part of the old servants' quarters but away from everyone else.

"You're just like the rest of them, Xander," Mum would say. "Never ever be afraid to pitch in and get your hands dirty to help out. You must always keep a little distance, though. You are their boss after all. Where you sleep, where you eat, how you address them. It earns respect and respect makes this place run all the smoother."

She had been right, of course, she usually was even if she really wasn't. Every time I made a decision I'd wonder whether she'd have approved. I wasn't sure I'd ever break that habit. Maybe one day, when the grief wasn't so very tangible. When father had died, I'd been upset, but it hadn't lasted that long, sadly. What I'd mourned was the loss of the opportunity to have a father, not him. He had never been very good at it.

The anger I had felt after his passing was in relation to not having a dad, rather than losing him. And that was a mind fuck in itself. Grieving for Mum had made me realize the difference. I missed her at the weirdest moments, the burning ball of sadness crept up on me at the most stupid and inconvenient times. I wasn't sure how to cope with it. Luckily I'd always been able to hold in the emotion then distract myself with something else. I couldn't let my weakness show.

I shook off my shoes and trousers and put them on the wooden chair at the end of my bed. Scrunching up my sweater, I threw it into the laundry basket sitting in the doorway to the bathroom. A quick stride over to the window to draw the curtains, then I hopped into bed. I could traverse the whole room in a few steps. It was basic, no frills, and it did me just fine. I only ever used it for sleeping anyway.

Most nights I'd fall into bed and straight to sleep but that night I found myself tossing and turning, haunted by India's startling green eyes and the remembrance of her body on top of mine. She was soft and warm, her curves fascinated me. My upbringing as a gentleman meant I kept my hands to myself but I imagined, there in my bed, what would have happened if I'd grabbed her and held her closer to me.

I could hear her gasp, see her pupils dilate and taste her lips as they mashed with mine. The conjured up images aroused me. I had to rip down my boxers and grab my cock. Fuck propriety, fuck expectations, I just wanted to fuck her, and what was the harm in indulging a little fantasy?

Dream hands burrowed up and under her shirt, molding her tits, rubbing circles with my thumbs, tracing the erect nubs, plucking them to feel her intake of breath on my lips. Pinching then and feeling her moan, my cock jumping in reaction to her response. In my fantasy I could have it any way I liked and I wanted to be on top.

Bodies rolled, I was between her thighs. No need to fumble with zippers, skirts and underwear—the fantasy allowed me to strip us in seconds, to hold her hands up above her head and watch her eyes widen when she realized what I was going to do.

Frenzied wanking in reality translated into rough hard fucking in my mind. Groans and grunts and tightening muscles squeezed me to my climax. It was her eyes, the lust, the expression in her face that pushed me over. My orgasm continued and her gaze fixed on me in my imagination. I was spent.

Suddenly tiredness took over me. I didn't have time to think about the return of my libido, which had been missing for months, if not years, or the implication of feeling such lust for a visiting journo, for a woman who would be in my life one minute then gone the next. Those were problems for another day.

Chapter Seven

India Grace

"Sleep well?" Mary asked when I dragged myself through the door to the shop. It looked like she'd been there a while. I wondered if she ever slept, if she ever looked anything less than perfectly prim.

"Yeah." I yawned. "Just not long enough."

"So, I was thinking you could start off doing some shelf stacking. We don't get many people through early on. I'll get you on a till later. Is that okay? That is the kind of thing you expect to do, isn't it?"

"Yeah, that's fine. These days I don't expect to do anything. When you've ended up waist-deep in a stinky fish pond fishing out gunk you start to expect anything, really."

"Oh, I remember that one. You didn't have a great time there, did you?"

"No, not really. I was used like unpaid labor for the whole three days I was there. I don't remember sleeping at all."

"Well, we'll be in for a higher score than Bertram's then. We've fed you and everything."

"Yes." I laughed. "Yes, you have."

"Okay, follow me. I want you to replenish the rapeseed oil shelf. It's one of our best sellers."

Moving bottles from trolley to shelf was actually quite a pleasant job. The gunk in the fish pond might have been the most disgusting job I'd ever been given to do but I'd had some thoroughly horrible experiences at other halls. I had been taken out on a pheasant shoot at one place. I understood the need to keep the bird numbers down but seeing the poor things shot down in their prime had made me sick to my stomach. I had been asked to join in, but I hadn't been able to. It just seemed like such a bleak thing to do, to purposefully set out to end an animal's life.

I'd watched livestock being slaughtered too. That wasn't at all pleasant, but being a steak and bacon lover it had given me an appreciation for where my meat came from. The slaughter process was clean and involved minimal pain. Before my dinner went through that for me I wanted it to have spent some time frolicking in fields and being properly alive.

"Well, this is weird," Mary muttered as I walked toward her, the till drawer open before her. "It's not adding up."

"Finished that, Mary," I shouted as I drew closer. She looked up at me.

"Okay, let me show you the till and how it works. I'll need a hand when it gets busy later. Harry and Jenny are both out working on the fencing today and the occasional lad we use is on holiday. And Phil only does the butchery. He can't operate the tills."

Phil—a rounded, smiling man in a red-striped pinny—waved at me with his cleaver from behind the harshly lit fridge displays then returned to creating lamb chops from a rich red carcass of meat.

The till wasn't difficult to get the hang of. I'd worked a bit of time in a supermarket, back when I'd dropped journalism. When Lord Mallard had died I hadn't been able to take it. I hadn't wanted anything else to do with the trade at all so I'd gone through a raft of odd jobs to make ends meet. Though they'd met in the way an old jacket does—briefly, just at the very ends.

"How long have you been here, Mary?" I asked when there was a lull in the demand for the tills. The shop was busy. Several people had told me they came in for a certain special item. Phil's lamb chops were extremely popular, as were the eggs. The business was clearly thriving.

"Oh, years." She shook her head. Her gray curls should have bounced but they seemed to stay perfectly rigid. She'd either had a very aggressive perm or an unhealthy addiction to hairspray. "I saw little Xander grow up and he's, what? Twenty-eight or something now? I must have been here for at least thirty-five years, what do you reckon, Phil?"

Mary waffled on a bit, but I didn't hear what was being said. What did she mean about seeing Xander grow up?

"I reckon Phil might be right, you know, might well be forty years." She nodded.

"Wow, that's some dedication," I declared. I had to get my head back in the game, concentrate on the article I was going to have to write.

"Oh, you know. I love this place, love the family, and what with all the troubles they've had, I've not had the heart to leave." She sighed.

"So the house is still in the hands of the Mallards? I thought Xander owned it."

"Yeah, that's right." Mary sighed. "I told Lady Mallard she needed to keep the name but she insisted on changing back to Patrick. Her husband died, I'm sure you know the story—you are old enough to know the story, aren't you?"

I nodded, slowly.

"Well, between you and me and the doorpost"—she nodded conspiratorially at Phil—"it was the best thing that happened to Mallard's. I know that sounds awful cruel and I'd never wish ill on anyone." She crossed herself fervently—a nun would have been impressed with her skill. "But he was a bad 'un. Ran this place down into awful debt. Got himself mixed up in all kinds of things he shouldn't. When Lady Mallard took over, things got so much better and, well, Xander's helped out since he was a kid too. I knew he'd make a great Lord Mallard. Shame he won't take the name back. I really think he should be proud of his family heritage."

"So." I took a deep breath in, tried to keep it calm. I held onto the countertop for dear life, lightheaded and hands shaking as I asked for confirmation of my worst fear. "Xander Patrick is Eustace Mallard's son?"

"Yes, yes he is. Poor mite was only young when his dad died, about twelve or thirteen, I think."

"How terrible." I gasped. I had to keep the conversation going—I couldn't let anyone know how petrified I was.

"Aye, awful it was. He coped admirably for his age and he's never once complained about the responsibilities he took on. I mean, him and his mum ran this place so well between them. He's barely held it together these past six months since Margaret passed on. I told him, he needs to have a proper time of mourning but he won't step back. He's got to always be in control, that one."

"His mum died?" I knew it, he'd told me, but the shock still had me in its grips.

"Yeah, cancer. Bloody awful it was. Mind you, once she found out she went quick. Least it wasn't a long, lingering experience, thank the Lord for small mercies."

I nodded, still rocked from the revelation. Why hadn't I found any indication that Xander was a Mallard?

"She'd have never let you on here, though, miss, she hated journalists of all kinds."

"Did she?"

"Yeah, blamed 'em for the death of her husband. You probably know the photo that got old Lord Mallard into trouble."

The image was seared into my brain. The sly smile of the prostitute, the bored, glazed look on Lord Mallard's face. My stomach churned so much I clutched at it, afraid I'd be sick.

"Margaret said it made him snap. Like, it didn't matter anymore if people knew." Mary finally looked over at me. "Oh, my dear, are you all right?"

"Yeah, I think I just need a bit of air."

"Go on, go on with you. I hope you're not coming down with something."

"No." I shook my head. "I'll be fine. Just get these odd dizzy spells. Something to do with my inner ear being off balance," I waffled, made it up. I didn't want people fussing around me.

"Okay, well, don't go far, will you?"

"I won't," I called over my shoulder and barreled out of the shop, knocking Gerald sideward.

"Watch where you're going!" he yelled and snarled at me. His placid face twisted into something ugly.

"Sorry." I gasped then carried on. I ran round to the back of the shop and collapsed to the floor beside a pile of discarded fruit boxes.

What the fuck am I going to do? I thought over and over again. I wanted to pack my bags and leave. Just grab my stuff and go, but what would that achieve? I'd be sacked. Maxine wouldn't stand for such a failure and I couldn't just make up the article on what information I'd already gleaned.

Or could I? Concoct an emergency and leave early. Just write them a glowing report made up from what I had experienced and all would be fine. I questioned that, though. It took time to get into the psyche of a place and I hadn't got there yet with Mallard's.

Some of my most glowing articles, full of praise and positivity, had resulted in barely any difference in revenue for the hall mentioned because they were just words. It was homes where I truly felt emotionally engaged that garnered the most success. And I couldn't do this half-heartedly. I'd already caused the downfall of the place. I didn't want to halt its recovery in its tracks too.

Then there was Xander. I liked Xander.

Dashing tears from my eyes, I took a long breath. No one had realized my connection to the infamous photo. It wasn't directly obvious. I'd gotten paid for the photograph and the credit had gone to the newspapers, not me. It would take some digging to find out that I was the person who'd taken that photo. I'd have to carry on regardless. I owed it to the place, to Xander, to carry on, write an amazing article and hopefully increase visitors. Mallard Hall deserved that from me. Xander deserved that from me. And nothing else. I couldn't let my stupid emotions get in the way.

Footsteps pulled me from my thoughts. Gerald approached with a box in his arms.

"Oh, Ms. Grace, I didn't know you were here, you startled me."

He hadn't jumped or gasped or shown any kind of surprise. Strange man.

"I'm just going. Had a bit of a funny turn and needed some fresh air. I'm okay now, though. Sorry if I scared you before." I pulled myself up and brushed down my jeans.

"No, no, it's okay, you startled me a little is all. Glad you're all right." He didn't want to engage in conversation and he shifted his body weight from one foot to the other as I watched. "Mary was worried, you better let her know you're okay."

"I will. Bye, Gerald," I replied.

He didn't even respond, I wondered what he was up to and what was in the box. Probably some old relic of time gone by that he wanted to stroke in privacy. Strange man, something about him disturbed me.

Mary kept me busy for the rest of the day—she really was a force of nature. After her shift in the shop each night she would go straight off to prepare the dinner for all the workers.

"We had a cook once upon a time but it was too much of an expense to keep on, so I volunteered to do it. I'm at a loose end from five anyway."

"Do you get paid for it?"

She looked at me awry, like I'd asked her to shoot a kitten. "No, no, not at all. I do it to keep the old place going."

"That's good of you." I smiled.

She shrugged and brushed it off like it was nothing.

"Do you need a hand at all?"

"Oh, no, it's fine. I like to keep the kitchen to myself, you know. See you later."

The staff at Mallard's really loved the place. It wasn't just a job for them, it was a calling. I made some notes up in my room then decided I couldn't hold my curiosity in anymore. I had to go and see the baby lamb. Xander might be there but I wasn't going to be able to avoid him. The next day I was due to interview him anyway. I'd have to face him sooner or later.

Harriet and her lamb were a vision of joy. The little lamb was trotting about quite confidently on her little hooves and stupidly long legs. Mum was fussing after her, bleating and nudging her offspring. It calmed my spirit. Who wouldn't feel better looking at such a contented scene?

I wasn't called to be a vet but whenever I looked back on that time I remembered it fondly and wondered how different my life would have looked if I'd continued my training. Not just as a vet but with Tom.

When I had gone home with him on the day I finished my placement, it had gone pretty much the way I'd expected at first. We had kissed and cuddled, gasped and groaned and pulled at each other's clothing until we'd both been close to bare.

"Can I spank you?" he had asked. "I've been thinking about it since the first day I met you."

I had agreed without much thought. I hadn't been experienced in sex and certainly not confident in myself. I had thought if I said no he'd have rejected me completely and I hadn't wanted that.

What I hadn't expected was to enjoy it. To find myself writhing across his lap, craving the next swat, the next stinging impact of hand on buttock. At first I had wanted it to stop, had been close to screaming out and ending it all, but then the pain had spiked to pleasure.

I couldn't say when my ouches turned into oohs of delight but I am sure Tom had worked it out because that's when he had started talking again.

"You like it, don't you?" he'd asked.

"Yes," I had eagerly acquiesced.

"Yes what?" he'd snapped. The next slap had been harder than those previously.

"Yes, I do." I had been confused, turned on and so silly and naïve.

"Sir. You should address me as Sir."

Another harsh swipe of his hand had provoked a scream but when the pain had eased and the pleasure had kicked in I'd remembered what I should say.

"Yes, Sir. I like it, Sir."

"Good girl," he'd purred.

I thought I heard the words out loud and it startled me back from my memories to reality.

"Oh, India, didn't see you there."

"Hey, Xander, just came to check in on them." I managed to speak and not trip over my tongue, which really was a miracle.

"Me too." He smiled. "They're doing well."

An awkward silence pulled out between us. I couldn't see any similarity between Xander and his dad. Xander's eyes were stunning blue—his father's had been dark, almost black, and tiny and cold. Even though Xander's were sharp blue they carried far more warmth than I'd glimpsed in the gaze of the old Lord Mallard.

"You all right, India?"

"What?" I'd been staring at him. *Oh God.* "Oh, yes, sure. I'm sorry, I was staring."

"Well, yeah, just a bit. Have I got something on my face?"

I shook my head, took a deep breath then explained myself. "No, it's just Mary told me you're Eustace Mallard's son. I didn't realize you were a Mallard, I was trying to see the resemblance."

There was something I couldn't tell Xander, something I'd never be able to tell him and I hoped he'd never find out. So I owed him the truth where I could provide it.

"Oh, well." Xander shrugged like he was trying to unseat awkwardness from his shoulders. "I don't really look like him much, no. I mean, I look more like Mum." He pulled a worn and thin, brown leather wallet from his pocket and flipped it open.

"Here's me and Mum. I was very little when this was taken, well, I mean, clearly."

The tiny photo was cracked and worn around the edges, but muted colors didn't hide the fact that mother and son shared the same bright blue eyes and jet black hair.

"She was very beautiful," I said, "and you look very much like her."

It wasn't just the coloring they shared. Their face shapes, their expressions were incredibly similar, even back then. Xander was just a toddler but he was instantly recognizable. Slim face, high cheekbones, wide eyes and a smile that glowed. Looking from the photo to Xander showed the same face with the burden of age, but the same intelligent curiosity shone through.

"She was stunning, could have been a model. Fiercely intelligent, stubborn too. Mum always knew just what to say."

He sighed so deeply. I wanted to hold him, the pain apparent in that anguished sound and his tortured face.

"I'm sorry for your loss, Xander." I squeezed his arm, just above the elbow. "My mum died a few years ago, I think I said. I still miss her every day but it gets easier to bear. The grief never leaves but the memories of the good things seem to come more easily to mind eventually."

He nodded, bit his bottom lip and breathed deeply. The poor guy was trying hard not to cry.

I slipped my arm around him to offer comfort.

"You do look very much like her," I said, not sure what to do. "The similarity is striking."

"People always commented on it. Still do. I don't look like my father at all. No wonder you didn't know that technically I'm Lord Mallard."

"Does this mean I have to curtsy when I see you?" I asked, hand still around him, feeling his warmth against me.

"No"—he grinned—"no, but you can call me 'Sir' if you want to."

Heat sizzled through me, centering deep in my pussy. Dear God, why did he have to say that of all things? "Okay, Sir." I tried to say it casually, like a joke, but the word caught in my throat, adding an urgency that I hadn't meant there to be.

"That's more like it." He chuckled. It was a throaty sound. I didn't know whether that was because he was as turned on as me or if it was a leftover from his grief. Either option made me uncomfortable.

Xander pulled away from me a little, and I dropped my arm to my side. It tingled, like I could still feel his heat there, his imprint.

"So yes, I'm Lord Mallard's son. I don't publicize it, I'm not really very proud of it, but it's true."

"I don't really know much about him, you know, just a bit, what I saw in the press." My casual demeanor didn't fool me, but I hoped he wouldn't pick up on my awkwardness.

"No, well, the press didn't tell the whole story, but it got the headlines right. I don't think about it, about him. How he ruined this place single-handedly. I choose to focus on how I can continue to build it back up, to continue my mother's legacy."

"A positive focus is always the best." I meant it. I'd spent so long dwelling on the negative things in my life I knew that didn't work. It just made existence bleak and painful.

"Yeah, yeah, I believe so." Xander closed his wallet and nodded purposefully.

"India, would you like to join me for dinner?"

"Oh, well—" There was a very good reason I should have said no. I'd been very, very sure that I shouldn't spend more time with Xander Patrick than was strictly necessary, but at that moment in time I couldn't think of any excuse. "Yes, that'd be lovely, thank you."

Chapter Eight

Xander Patrick

"Great." I smiled. "Great, good, well, come on then."

Why did I ask her to dinner? God, I'd already made a complete fool of myself. All she'd done was look at me a bit funny then somehow I'd ended up virtually in tears telling her about Mum. *She won't put that in her article, will she?*

"Erm, India, I'm sure this is a silly question but you won't put any of this – this personal stuff in your write-up, will you?"

She shook her head. "No, no, of course not."

"Good. I mean, I thought you'd say that, it was a bit of a daft question."

"The only silly question is the one you don't ask."

"Fair enough. Come on then, let's head back to the hall. The girls seem happy enough."

"They are a vision of contentment." India sighed. "Makes even my jaded journo heart melt to see them."

I'm sure that she was only joking but that reminder that she was a journalist was timely. I'd just spilt my guts to someone with connections to the media. She could ruin me if she felt so inclined. I believed her when she said it would stay out of *Good Manors*, but would she sell the story to the tabloids?

"Do you write for anyone else?" I asked, walking alongside her back toward the hall.

"No, I don't. I used to be a freelancer, wrote and took photos for loads of different papers and magazines but, well, it didn't agree with me, let's put it like that. I work exclusively for *Good Manors* now."

Did she realize why I'd asked that question? All I seemed to do was insult her.

"That pays all right then?" I cringed inwardly the moment I said it. One day I'd remember to think before opening my gob.

"Not bad. I mean, I won't be buying my own stately manor any time soon, but I get by."

"Sorry, India, that was a really rude thing to ask."

"Not really." She smiled. "I know why you're nervous around me. I've gotten used to it over time. You're worried whatever you tell me will end up in tomorrow's newspapers."

"No!" I denied. "Not at all."

"You don't have to pretend, Xander, I understand. It comes with my profession."

"Okay, well, I don't mean to be like that." I shrugged. "I really don't."

"Don't sweat it." She shrugged, setting her long, brunette hair bouncing. "I'm used to it, but I *am* telling you the total truth. I only write for *Good Manors* and I will only put information relevant to the manor into my article."

"I believe you." And I did, even if the warning bells Mum had planted in my psyche were ringing at full pelt. "I do believe but you can understand, my family have suffered a bit at the hands of the press."

Her cheeks flushed and something flashed through her eyes. Anger maybe.

"Sure, sure." India nodded.

"God, I've put my foot in it again." I sighed.

"No, it's fine. I understand. Your family was treated badly. I left that side of the media a long time ago. My conscience couldn't take it. People need some privacy. We all have secret parts of our lives we want to keep to ourselves."

"I mean, my father was up to no good and he probably would have run the hall into the ground anyway but Mum said he went crazy once those photos came out. He went into overdrive. People knew he was bad, so he played up to it. Mum really wasn't very keen on the press. That's why we've not even had a local newspaper photographer at any of our launches. My mum just didn't trust them. She couldn't see the good in it."

We'd reached the drive in front of the manor, and she stopped in her tracks.

"I wouldn't be surprised if whoever took that photo regretted it deeply." Her words seemed heavy and poignant. I'd really upset her.

"Of course, none of this is a judgment on you and just because Mum was so anti-press doesn't mean that I am. You're here, aren't you?"

India nodded.

"So I'm going to shut up before I upset you even further. Now, follow me, dinner should pretty much be done."

"Sorry, Xander. I get a bit touchy about the subject. I know journalism has its bad side. I avoid that, though, like the plague."

"I know." I let her walk in before me then once we were inside I signaled for her to go past the staircase. "I really do. You're one of the good guys. Hell, you're an angel as far as I'm concerned. Without you I might not have a lovely lamb in my life today."

"Oh, that was nothing." She chuckled and my heart swelled with relief. There was still a chance I hadn't completely turned her against me with my stupid talk.

"In here." I indicated a doorway. "This is the staffroom for the house tour folks."

"Ah, right. Why are we in here?"

"At the end there is my little office. In an evening, when the staff have left, I use the rest of the staffroom too. I can use the little kitchen to make my dinner. There's even a sofa and a TV."

Of all the rooms in the house this one was the most modern, the one least like a stately home.

"So you spend your time in what I'm guessing is the only place in this whole manor that doesn't feel like it hails from over a hundred years ago."

"Yep, got it in one." I set to pulling out plates and cutlery.

"Want me to put those out?" she asked.

"Yeah, please."

"Smells great in here," she commented, laying out the table mats and cutlery on the plain wooden table.

I'd have liked to have got something more contemporary but we had an old but not ancient wooden one already. I couldn't justify buying new when we had something that would suffice.

"It does, doesn't it?" I lifted the lid from the slow cooker and inserted a ladle. "I can't take all the credit. This baby does all the work." I tapped the ladle on the edge of the Crockpot. "I just stuff the ingredients in."

"Doesn't Mary cook for you?" India pulled out a chair and sat down at the table.

"Oh, she'd like to." I chuckled. "And she used to, but she's a bit of a control freak and if I was more than a few minutes late to dinner she'd lay into me. So in the end I decided it was better for my health to prepare my own meals. She's still not happy about it, but I'm the boss so she doesn't complain about it very often anymore. Just most days. Not every day."

"I can quite imagine." India moved her fork minutely to the left to straighten it. "She's an interesting character, isn't she?"

"Oh yes." I lifted a ladle of steaming stew and carefully poured it into one of the bowls in front of me. "She really is. The longest serving member of staff here, you know."

"Really, I thought that might be Gerald."

"No." I continued to serve, trying hard not to let my hand shake. The woman was yards away from me but I still felt her energy, her presence, and it disturbed me. "No, Gerald's relatively new here actually. Arrived a year or so ago."

"Oh, he knows so much about the place I thought he'd worked here forever."

"No, he learnt all that as a paying visitor. He was well known, in fact. The only annual pass holder who'd visit at least once a week without fail. Sometimes the old guide would let Gerald lead the tour when his arthritis was playing up, he was that good. So when Fred retired it seemed natural to offer Gerald the job. He leaped at the chance."

I walked over to the table with the bowls in my hands and placed one in front of India.

"Well, I am surprised, I thought he was more established than that."

"Feels like he's always been here." I pulled out my chair and sat down. "Though not everyone likes him."

"No?" India dipped her spoon into the bowl before her.

"No, he's quite, well… How do I put it?" I dipped my own spoon in and brought the steaming contents to my lips. The aroma of sweet beef and rich gravy enveloped me. "He's a bit of an acquired taste."

"I must admit, there's something about him that gives me the creeps a bit. I don't know what it is."

"I know what you mean, I wasn't sure about employing him for the same reason but he got on so well with the other members of staff and his knowledge was so good, he didn't even need any training. It was a no-brainer to give him the job really."

"Oh yeah, he's clearly very good at what he does. Do the tourists like him?" India sipped at the stew in her spoon then delicately nibbled on a piece of beef.

Everything she did seemed elegant to me. I shoveled another spoonful of food into me. I was starving, I'd not eaten anything all day.

"Most of them do, yeah. A few of the older ones who remember Fred aren't that taken with him but mostly the visitors seem to like him. Well, there's always people going on his tours and some of them are regulars who come back time and time again."

"That's really important." India nodded. "It's one thing getting new customers through the door but another entirely to keep them coming back. It's a sign of a good and well run business when there's return custom."

Conversation flowed well, which was a relief after I'd managed to insult her profession so heavily. She made me laugh—how refreshing. I thought I'd forgotten how to.

"Do you need a hand with the pots?" India asked as she let her spoon fall into her empty bowl.

"Oh, no, I'll be fine. There's not much to do." I picked up the bowls and took them over to the sink.

"Well, it'll be done all the quicker if I help. Pass us a tea towel."

"Fine, fine, if you insist, the tea towel's tucked in here." I moved away from the front of the sink so she could take the towel from over the handle.

"Well, it's only fair. That was a delicious meal."

"Glad you enjoyed it." I smiled. "You can join me again tomorrow if you like."

"Sure," she replied easily, "that'd be great."

"I've not even told you what's on the menu yet."

"Oh, I'm sure it'll be tasty." She reached over to pick up the bowl I was just putting down after washing and her fingers touched mine. I let go quicker than I should and the bowl dropped. I went to catch it but she was faster and got there first, grabbing it before it smashed down onto the counter.

"Good catch." I sighed. "Sorry about that, was a bit slippery."

"I'm impressed with my reflexes." She laughed. "I didn't realize they were that good."

"Well, I'm glad they are or I'd have Mary on my back for breaking it. She's an absolute terror about stuff like that."

"That doesn't surprise me." India chuckled. "She seems like she wants everything just so."

When we finished washing and wiping I went to pick up the pile of cleaned items but India made the same move and we ended up chest to chest.

"Oh, I'm sorry—"

"No, no, my fault." I grabbed her arms instinctively to steady her. "I seem to be extra clumsy tonight."

"I'm getting under your feet," she replied. "I should get out of your way."

"I quite like you in my way, India." Why I said that I didn't know. Her presence must have addled my brain.

"Really?" She looked to the side and pushed at her hair, hooking it behind her ear. She was blushing.

"Yes, well, it's good to have someone around who seems to be on the same wavelength as me. I mean, it seems like you are. Not that you maybe want to be. Oh God, I should shut up now, shouldn't I?"

"Maybe a good idea, Xander, but I know what you mean. I'm drawn to you myself."

"You are?" I'd not let go of her, she'd not moved away from me. There was a tension in the air that seemed to keep us held in place.

"Yes, I am. I probably shouldn't be, considering my career and all, but I can't seem to help myself."

Did she lift up to my lips or did I lean over toward her? Maybe we both moved. It was like I'd woken from a dream and I was already deep in the kiss, my arms wrapped around her, our mouths joined, our breath shared between us. All I could hear was the raging thump of my heart, all I could smell was the light rose and citrus of her scent, all I experienced was her. I was completely immersed in India.

Then the door creaked and we jumped apart.

"Oh, I'm glad you're here, Mr. Patrick, I've been looking at the figures again and it's wrong, all wrong." Mary walked into the room, head down, eyeing a piece of paper in her hand. India coughed.

"Oh, India, hello dearie, I wondered where you'd got to."

"Hi, Mary, Xander invited me to dinner. I was just leaving."

"Righto, dear. I'll see you in the morning."

"Goodnight, Mary." She headed past her to the door. "Goodnight, Xander."

"Night, India." I waved. My heart plummeted. What must she be thinking? What could have happened if Mary hadn't disturbed us when she had?

"We did a full stocktake, Mr. Patrick, and we're down two hundred quid. I can't work it out at all."

"I don't know." I scraped my fingers through my hair as I held the stocktake figures in my other hand. "Are you sure someone isn't nicking?"

"I don't think so, I really don't. I mean, it's usually me on the till then it might be Harry or Jenny but Phil never goes near the till and in the last couple of days it's only been me on the till and I'm not on the take, Mr. Patrick."

"I know, Mary, I know. Is someone taking stock then?"

"That might be it but there's no firm evidence of it. If they're taking it, they're taking from the items we produce on the farm. We keep precise numbers and details on the bought in stock but maybe we're a bit less thorough with the home produced stuff."

"Can you keep a closer eye on that then, Mary?"

"Aye, I can at least try." She nodded.

"And keep an eye on Harry and Jenny. You might have been on the till lately, but they've still got access to it through the day. You've not been on the tills all day, surely."

"No, young India took over for a bit, but I'm sure it wasn't her."

"No, I'm sure too. This problem started long before India arrived, but someone could have got to the money while she was in charge. She's not used to the job like you, Mary."

"We need to do something, Xander. This has been going on for three months now. If we continue to lose so much, we'll not be able to keep the shop going. It'll go from making us a great profit to being a drain. We're not far off it, Xander, we're not."

"I know." I sighed. "Maybe we need to install some video cameras?"

Mary's face soured, her lips pursing, her eyes darkening.

"Well, you know what I think about that, Mr. Patrick." Mary most often called me Mr. Patrick when she was mad at me. "But apart from it being a complete and utter invasion of privacy it would be very costly to buy. We can't afford it."

"If we keep losing money, we'll have to do something, Mary. It makes me sick to my stomach to think someone, somewhere at Mallard's, is stealing from me."

"I know." Mary gripped my arm. "Me too, me too."

"Thanks for all you do." I smiled at her. "Without you, I'd have gone under already."

"Oh, hush." She shook her head, spots of red highlighting her pale cheeks. "I just do my job."

"Your job is vital to Mallard's, vital to me. I'm glad you're here."

"Always, Xander, always. Mallard's is my home." She squeezed my arm then let go.

"Just check those figures over, check I've worked it out right. I'll do what I can to tighten things up in the shop tomorrow."

She headed toward the door then stopped partway there.

"Ooh, what is India doing tomorrow? I don't think we worked it out."

"Well, she's done the tour with Gerald and spent the day in the shop with you. She could do with experiencing the farm and the gardens."

"I'll talk to Graham in the morning then. She can join the groundsmen tomorrow."

"Yeah, I need to meet her, too, she's doing some kind of interview. Get her to come to my office at four tomorrow, will you?"

"Yes, boss, will do. I know the article she does for us will bring in the crowds, Xander."

"I think you're right, Mary. Well, I hope you're right." I sighed.

"I'm always right." She winked at me, her soft face wrinkling with mischief. "You should know that by now."

"Oh, I do, Mary, I do." I grinned. "I never forget it."

She laughed and shook her head. "See you later."

"Bye, Mary."

Chapter Nine

India Grace

We'd kissed. I was supposed to be avoiding him, trying to keep out of his way, and we'd kissed. I'd agreed to share a meal with him and somehow that had led to lip-locking. And God knows where it would have ended up if Mary hadn't intervened when she had.

I lay in bed, blankets cuddled up tight under my chin, thinking it all over. The meal had been nice, we'd talked about all sorts of things, not just the hall but hobbies and art, even mentioned football at one point and strayed into the realm of politics. Xander was a good conversationalist. It was a surprise, but I found myself feeling quite relaxed in his presence.

Once I'd been sure he had no idea of my connection to his father, I'd found it surprisingly easy to relax. I even enjoyed talking to him. I didn't have many friends. I talked to folks at work but we didn't spend any social time together, except the Christmas party, and I rarely attended that.

I really shouldn't have let him kiss me. Although, to be truthful, I could have kissed him. I didn't remember those finer details. I remembered how his mouth felt against mine, how his lips had been hot and malleable, his body hard against mine. I remembered his musk, light and spicy. We'd kissed but how that had started I had no real clue.

How was I going to face him? At least there was only one last day to spend at the manor. One day, another night then I could go home.

* * * *

My lips danced over Xander's, I pulled him close to me. I could feel his body heat, his hands resting on my hips, but then everything was cold, oh so very cold, and the hands on my hips fell away and when I looked again it was his father's corpse I was kissing.

My screams morphed into a gasp of shock, the body was gone and a newspaper rested between my hands. I looked down and the front page was a giant photo of Xander and me kissing.

"I can't look at you, you dirty, evil fucking bitch." Xander's face contorted with anger. "You killed him!"

I woke with a vision of Xander's face and grief etched into my mind. There was no way I could let myself give in to my desires once more. There was no good way that any kind of intimacy between Xander and me could end well.

* * * *

"Morning, India." Mary stood at the bottom of the stairs, bright red waterproof top and trousers contrasting with yellow wellington boots.

"Xander said to send you out with the groundsmen today. Have you got a waterproof?"

"Yes, I have."

"Nip up and get it, love, you're going to need it. I'll take you over to where the guys are working before I get to the shop. Make sure you wrap up warm too. The weather's taken an awful turn."

I didn't realize just how cruel Xander was until I got outside. To say it was raining was more than an understatement. Some vengeful god was raging in the skies, throwing buckets of freezing cold water at the earth, the contents of which seemed to be focused on me. To add insult to injury, the winds were joining in too, battering the waterproof around me, snatching the hood from my head, exposing my hair to the lashing rain.

"Awful weather, isn't it? I wouldn't blame you if you refused to go out in this." Mary battled into the wind beside me.

"No, I need to do it—this is what the staff have to deal with. It's what I have to deal with."

"Well, good luck." She came to an abrupt stop and glanced around, squinting into the rain. "Oh, there they are, up in the back corner there."

I squinted in the direction she pointed. I could just make out a huddle of bodies toward the far end of the lawn.

"You get off to the shop, Mary. I know where they are now."

"Are you sure? I'll walk over with you if you want."

"No, it's fine, you get in the dry and the warm." I really didn't want the poor woman to get any wetter.

"Well, okay then. Oh, Mr. Patrick wants to see you at four."

I looked blankly at her.

"You're interviewing him or something, yes?"

"Oh, right, yes, of course."

"He said you should go to his office at four."

"Right then, thanks, Mary, I will."

"And don't let Graham bully you. If it gets too much for you get indoors. It's not your job to be out in this."

"Thanks, Mary. I can look after myself."

"I know you can. See you later, India."

"Bye, Mary."

I didn't turn to watch her go. Instead I put my head down and forged forward. When I reached the three bodies, they ignored me. They were focused on a length of wood. One was holding it in place, another hammering nails into it and another held the post of the existing fencing in place.

Once the hammering had ended I shouted up, "Hello there!"

No one looked at me.

"I said, hello, I'm India, I'm here to help."

Finally the man doing the hammering looked up.

"Oh, you did come then," he proclaimed gruffly. "We thought the shower might keep you indoors."

I had the measure of Graham within a few moments. He thought that strength was all physical and that he was the top dog. An alpha male—in his own mind, anyway.

"I wasn't going to let the weather stop me experiencing all the manor has to offer. What can I do to help?"

Graham pulled back his lips and sucked air between his teeth. "I'm not sure there's any light duties need doing today."

I wasn't going to rise to his barbs. I knew his type, he was digging for a reaction.

"Well, what are you doing? I'm here now, I might as well help."

"We're checking all the perimeter fences," one of the other green-clad figures said.

I was a little bit surprised to find it was Jenny.

"Now Harriet's had her babe," Jenny continued, "Xander said it's a priority that the whole place is enclosed properly."

"Yeah," the other figure spoke up. He was testing the repair Graham had made. "We've done over by the barns already."

When I realized it was Harry, I found myself blushing. My cheeks heated as I remembered the scene from the other night.

"Bloody hell, you two, I can speak, you know." Graham humphed.

"Sorry, boss," the duo said in perfect synchronicity.

"Well, since you're here I suppose you can go check the wire fence up at the back there."

Graham pointed farther up the gardens, to the bushes.

"Where is it, behind the shrubbery?"

"Yes, it marks the back of the property." He bent down, opened a toolbox and passed me a roll of wire, some red duct tape and wire cutters. "If there's any gaps block 'em up. If there's any areas that look weak mark them with the red tape. I'll assess the damage at a later point and replace anything that needs replacing."

"Okay, no problem." I took the proffered items.

"Keep following the fence, it goes right around the estate. I don't imagine you'll cover all of it today, but you should manage a sizeable amount. Me and Tweedledum and Tweedledee here will work on the internal fences."

"Okay, I've got to go and see Xander at four, I'm interviewing him. So I'll bring you your tools back before then."

"Make sure you do," he grumbled then turned his back on me. Clearly Graham hadn't got the message about being nice to me. I wouldn't hold Graham against the whole of Mallard Hall, as much as I might enjoy cutting him down to size. I couldn't risk anything negative in my report. I had to give it a glowing review and appease my guilty conscience.

"Will you be all right on your own, India?" Jenny shouted up, and Graham shot her a look filled with dagger-sharp insinuation.

"I'll be fine, thanks, Jenny."

"But Xander says we shouldn't work on our own, for health and safety."

"She's only looking at the damn fence, it's not like she's really doing any proper work."

I took a deep breath and clenched my fist. What an obnoxious man.

"But what if she gets hurt? No, I think I should go with her, boss, to be safe. You don't really need me here anyway. You were complaining about me two minutes ago."

Graham clearly didn't like that he'd been boxed into a verbal corner, and by a woman no less. I could see his mind whirring. I was almost convinced I could hear it too, the cogs grinding together.

"Fine, you girlies go off and leave us men to do the real work."

Harry didn't look very impressed.

"Whatever you say, boss." Jenny nodded, turned then beckoned to me.

We walked away from the guys toward where I could only assume we'd find the fence.

"Sorry about Graham. He's a bit of a tosser. He's a very good gardener, though."

"No worries." I was slightly shocked by Jenny's tone but I tried not to let it show. "I've met many men like Graham over the years. It's not worth letting them get to you."

"Too right," she agreed. "Harry isn't thrilled to be stuck with him but he didn't want you going off on your own."

"Harry was worried about me?"

"Yeah." She nodded. "He knew it wasn't right to send you off on your own. He's very strong on health and safety is Harry."

"Well, that's very good of him, I'll be sure to thank him later."

"He told me to volunteer to go with you. He would have done but Graham would have teased him something chronic. He's really childish like that."

"Yeah, you don't say," I scoffed.

We'd reached the protection of the shrubbery and I could feel just how cold my cheeks were. They were stinging from being in the wind. Jenny walked us parallel with the bushes.

"There's a break in the foliage somewhere round here. Oh yeah, Graham's a wanker. No one really likes working with him at all— Ah, here it is."

It was even drier within the shrubbery, a shelter away from the storm.

"Do you like working at Mallard's?" I asked.

"Oh yeah, it's proper good." She took the wire and the snips then passed me the red tape. "I get to do all sorts and mostly folks are nice. With a couple of exceptions."

"Who?"

"Well, they have a letter of the alphabet in common and you've only just seen one of 'em."

It didn't take me long to work out she meant Graham and Gerald.

"Are you enjoying your time here?" she asked, taking a length of wire and measuring it against a gap in the fence.

"Yeah, I am. It's a lovely place and I've had a very warm welcome from most people."

"Oh, good. Mary says if you put a good write-up in your posh mag it'll get loads more folks here. I hope so."

"I hope so too, Jenny." I smiled.

"If Mr. Patrick has to lose staff I'll be the first out. Only started work here a few months back. Me dad supplies the shop with asparagus and apples and other artisan seasonals. I used to help deliver 'em. One day Mary was overrun at shop and I asked me dad if I could stop on and help her, like. Well, he said yes and I helped out that whole weekend when Cheryl was ill. She never came back so Mr. Patrick offered me a job."

"And here you are. Is your dad happy you work here?"

"Oh aye, I've got three younger brothers all working on the farm. I'm one less mouth to feed."

"You live here, don't you?"

"Yep, mostly. I do go home sometimes, in the winter over the holidays when there's not so much to do, like. But there's not really room for me there now. Callum has to sacrifice his room when I go home and he doesn't like it."

"So it works well for you, staying here, then."

"Yeah, it costs me a chunk of my wage but I get food and lodgings and I don't have to pay bills. I've never been very good with stuff like that. Working out bills and shit."

I bit off a piece of tape and wrapped it around an area that was rusted.

"But you work in the shop, I thought you'd be good with numbers."

I'd never been Miss Marple but I couldn't resist that line of enquiry. If I could find out who was on the take, it'd be another boost for Mallard's.

"Oh, the till does all the hard work. I just scan the barcodes or weigh the stuff and put the code in. No real maths required."

I didn't see a change in Jenny's demeanor. She was very open and I couldn't help liking her. I couldn't believe she was the mastermind behind the shop scandal.

"I'm not so good with numbers myself. Words and images are my thing."

"You're very good, miss. Harry was showing me some of your articles and pictures and stuff when we found out you were coming. They have your magazines in the main reception of the hall, you know. Mr. Patrick keeps the old ones in the staffroom."

"Thank you, Jenny. I do my best."

"Have you taken much photos?" she asked.

"No, not many so far," I replied with a smile at her unique approach to the English language. "I've got some general ones of the hall and I got a great one of Mary yesterday—she's laughing with a swede in her hand. I'm pretty sure I'm going to use it."

"Would you take a pic of me, miss? I know I'm not so very pretty, like, but I'd like a photo." At this she looked around conspiratorially. "For Harry. For his birthday. I'm making this picture frame out of twigs,

I'm weaving 'em together. It looks great but I need a photo to put in it and I don't have none of me."

"Not a one?"

She shook her head. "Nah, Dad brought us up. Mum died when I was little and he never thought of things like photographs. We don't have any at all."

"Of course I'll take a photo for you. I can take a photo of you and Harry together if you like?"

"That'd be good, you can say it's for your article, can't you, and then he won't know."

"Yeah, meet me at the bottom of the main stairs tomorrow morning and I'll take some photos before I go. I can post them to you when I've developed them."

"Oh, that's so good of you, thank you, miss."

"Call me India." I grinned and secured another strip of red around a stretched area of wire. "So are you and Harry an item then?" I tried to sound casual and not to think of the stables and the evidence I'd seen there.

"Yeah." She sighed. It was so sweet and completely not the kind of noise I expected her to make. "I fell for him the moment I met him, he's so gorgeous. I didn't think he'd look twice at me but you know, he did and we're dead good together. We don't let on to people, though—we work together and it might not look very professional. Neither of us wants to lose our jobs."

"No, I understand. But I'm sure it's fine. Xander seems a reasonable man and as long as you're both doing your work, it shouldn't really matter."

"I guess you're right, miss—I mean India—maybe we'd be okay, but it's kinda fun keeping it a secret. Oh, what's this? Blimey, this is a huge gap."

She was right, the wire fence wasn't just twisted or worn away—a whole chunk of it looked like it had been removed.

"We'll have to get something to block that up for now. Will you mark it out with red tape and I'll go and find summat. Gee wiz, it leads right out onto the road too, that's dangerous that is."

The more time I spent with Jenny the less I could see her as a swindler and a fraudster. I still couldn't determine who was taking the takings but I was certain it wasn't her. She kept me company all day and we were firm friends by the time I had to leave to interview Xander.

I barely had time to change out of my sodden jeans before I had to meet him. I didn't have time to ponder what to wear, so I just threw on my favorite long red skirt and the first clean T-shirt I pulled out of my bag then raced down to the staffroom and on to Xander's office.

"Hi." I gasped. "Sorry if I'm a bit late."

"It's all right." He waved at the chair on the opposite side of the desk. "I've been busy anyway."

"Yes, so was I. I've been out fixing the fencing."

"Oh, you've met Graham then." Xander hunched his shoulders and winced.

"Yeah, he's erm, interesting."

"He's not done anything to upset you, has he? Because if he has he'll be out on his backside, I don't care how good he is with Gran's roses or that he cuts the lawn just right. I've given him enough warnings."

"No, no, he wasn't exactly the most charming employee but don't sack him on my behalf. I spent most of my time with Jenny, she's lovely."

"She is." Xander smiled. "She's going out with Harry, you know."

My jaw dropped. "What? You're not meant to know—"

Xander laughed loudly. "I know, but they're not very subtle, God love 'em. I keep pretending, though. I think they get a thrill out of keeping it a secret."

"Well, I'd worked it out and I've only been here a few days. They are pretty obvious."

"Have you enjoyed your time here?" Xander asked. It sounded like an innocent and kind of obvious question but I sensed an undercurrent—or maybe I put that in because all I could think about was the kiss we'd shared.

"Sure." I nodded and coughed. "Yeah, I've had fun. People have been kind." I was convinced my cheeks were the same color as my skirt. I couldn't look him in the eye.

"Good, good. Well, I guess it's your turn to ask the questions."

"Yes, sure. And I need to take some photos too if you don't mind."

"I'm not sure." He hunched up in his seat. "I'm not very comfortable with that."

"Well, okay then, no problem. I just thought it would be good to get a photo of the latest Lord Mallard to go with my article, but never mind, I can use others."

"I've spent so long out of the public eye, I don't really want to be put back into it."

"No, it's fine, I understand. Yes, no worries."

I scrabbled with my notepad and waved my pen above it. He didn't trust me as much as I'd thought. I worked through my solid list of questions. Nothing too probing or heavy. Xander was clipped in his answers. Even though I tried to coax him out of his shell, to tell me more, he resisted my journalistic charms. It irked me.

"Well, I think that's it." I finally gave up. I was more likely to pull Excalibur from the stone than to get a genuine, heartfelt response from Xander Patrick. "Thanks for that, Mr. Patrick."

"I think you can call me Xander now, India." His tone was clipped.

I cringed. I felt like he was telling me off.

"Sure, Xander." I smiled and scrambled out of the battered plastic chair. "Are you positive I can't take any photos? I mean, you look good behind that desk."

"Well, thanks," he replied with a wink. "But no, I still don't want my face to appear in the media."

"Okay." I turned to face the door without saying anything more. I wanted to be free of the office, of his gaze. I'd only do something stupid if I stayed.

"You're still joining me for dinner tonight, aren't you?" he asked as I grabbed the door handle.

Shit. I'd forgotten I'd agreed to that. I turned slowly and hoped a good excuse would leap to mind.

"Well, I have a lot to write up. I like to get all my notes sorted while still on location then I can ask any questions if they crop up."

"Sure, I understand, but you still have to eat, right? Meet me here at seven."

He didn't ask, he commanded. I found myself responding instinctively.

"Yes, Sir." I blushed, smiled and tried to cover my faux pas with a shaky wink to show I was being funny. "Okay, I'll see you then."

"Bye, India. Wear something pretty, I'm cooking something special. It is your last night, after all."

"Okay." I nodded. "See you later." I just wanted out of the room before my face exploded. God that man turned me on and infuriated me in equal measure. Add to that the deep and abiding guilt that rested in the pit of my stomach every time I looked at him and I was surprised I didn't throw up at his feet with the nerves of it all.

It wasn't until I was back in my room that I thought over what he'd said.

"Something pretty?" I mimicked to the thin air. "How rude."

My style of dress was a little bit out there but that had really sounded like an insult. Maybe he didn't regard a bright pink skull with falsies to be pretty—that was what adorned the black T-shirt I'd picked up to throw on. Clearly, he was telling me to smarten up my act, the bastard. Well, I'd show him.

Chapter Ten

Xander Patrick

"Idiot, idiot, idiot," I cried and slammed my head down onto the table in front of me. Why the hell had I said 'wear something pretty'? She had been wearing something pretty. I was convinced she'd think I was insulting her. I wasn't. All I wanted was her to dress up a bit because I had plans that involved a far more impressive location for her last night's meal than the one of the previous night. I wanted to make a grand gesture but I'd ballsed it up in true Mallard tradition.

She hadn't said no, though. So I had to continue as planned and trust she'd turn up. I'd argued with myself all day over it. I was torn in two. Mum would have majorly disliked India. Not because of her personality but because of her career, and every time I looked at her I couldn't help but think about that. My mum was the only person in my life I had ever totally trusted.

"They're cunning, son," she'd said. "They'll do anything at all to convince you they're different, that they're nice as pie and will never do anything to hurt you but the next day your dirty underwear will be all over the tabloids. It's not worth the heartache, darling. Always be vigilant and never, ever trust anyone in the media."

I'd found it easy to believe her then because I'd never met a member of the media. Mum had kept them all away from me and from Mallard's full stop. I'd believed her, instinctually I'd known she was right. Dad had never been perfect but if that photo hadn't been leaked maybe he would have changed his life around and I'd have had a full and loving family, but it had been leaked and Dad had never had the opportunity to better himself.

India confused me. She was so sincere and kind and enthusiastic. She'd given her time and expertise to deliver Harriet's baby and refused all offers of payment. Mary liked her and she was a good judge of character. I'd even spent some time looking through her old articles in *Good Manors* and I hadn't found anything at all that would be considered sleazy or in any way shock journalism.

I wanted India Grace and I battled with that because I wasn't sure my mother would have approved. How sad was that. Mum wasn't even around and she was still dictating who I saw and what I thought. I loved her to bits but she had always been controlling, there were no two ways around it.

I only had to think of Ariana to realize it. Ariana had first worked for us back in the day and she'd been beautiful. Eighteen-year-old me had been captivated by her and not very subtle either, because as much as I had tried to keep our trysts a secret from my mum she had eventually found out, and the next day Ariana had been sacked. I never saw her again.

"She could have been the love of my life, Mother," I'd yelled.

"No, dear. She was just easy. You're worth much more than that common girl, you're a lord, for God's sake. No, I know what's best for you."

I hadn't spoken to her for a fortnight after that.

I pulled out my best suit—jet black and neatly pressed—and remembered the last time I'd worn it, at the gala opening of the Hall. It had been the first time I'd been in the place when it was bustling with people. The party we'd held had been huge and Mum had invited all the influential people in the area and some from farther afield.

She had tried hard to match me up with a woman who had some vague connection to royalty but I hadn't had any of it. Mum hadn't been impressed. She had accused me of making a fool out of her.

"I can't pretend to like someone I don't, Mum."

She had sighed and shaken her head. Her years had lain on her and she'd looked tired.

"You'll be amazed what you can do when you have to," she'd said. "After all, I married your father, didn't I?"

And that had been her trump card. I had deigned to make a date with the young girl in question based solely on my mother's desire for me to. It hadn't ended well.

I had to face my life on my own now. Mum was gone and I had to make my own decisions. I tied up my black tie and pulled it tight. I'd made up my mind. I was going to have India Grace and mark her as mine. Even if it only happened the once, I was going to make her mine. I needed to feel her against me, flesh to flesh. I wouldn't be able to settle until I had. I wouldn't be able to continue without trying.

She was probably going to out and out refuse me but since she was leaving the hall the next day and very unlikely to come back, I wasn't going to lose much more than a bit of face. Mum couldn't control me any longer. I had to make my own decisions and take the consequences. I only hoped they'd be good ones.

I got everything ready for what I hoped would be a date and a successful one at that, then rushed along to the staffroom to wait for India.

She kept me waiting for thirty minutes.

"Sorry I'm late," she purred on entering the room. "It takes a rather a while for me to get pretty."

"Wow." I was close to speechless. She was naturally gorgeous and didn't need anything to enhance that but she wore the most striking dress in a scarlet velvet that hugged her curves and showed off her pale flesh at bosom and thigh. "Just wow." I shook my head.

What am I doing?

She looked like the cat who'd got the cream. She stood defiantly, like she was challenging me to a duel. I was at once petrified and highly turned on. This woman wasn't going to roll over and surrender.

Pearls dangled from her ears and surrounded her neck. I was transfixed as she ran a finger across the collar of white beads at her throat, making me think of other white, creamy droplets as she showed off the scarlet of her nails.

"We're not eating in here tonight." I smiled. "I thought we'd really push the boat out as it's your last night here."

"Lead the way, then." She almost sounded disinterested but the glint in her eye gave her away.

"I only asked you to wear a pretty dress, India, not one that was prone to give me a heart attack."

"I like to go beyond a man's expectations." She winked.

"Oh, you certainly did that."

I led her down the corridor, her little heels click, click, clicking all the way to the dining room.

She gasped when we entered and it was my turn to smirk. I'd set up a smaller table by the fireplace and put candles on a bright white tablecloth then I'd pulled up two of our most opulent chairs. The upholstery matched her dress. The logs crackled in the grate and set a romantic glow around the room. I'd lit the candelabras along the huge state table but that was the only light, and it flickered and highlighted the polished silver and the beautifully detailed gold floral pattern on the dark red flocked wallpaper.

"Well, they didn't have electric lights back in the day, so I thought we'd keep things authentic." I captured her cold fingers and led her over to the table. I pulled back a chair and helped her sit. "Champagne?"

"Yes, please," she replied.

I walked over to the side table and retrieved a bottle from the ice bucket then deftly popped the cork.

"It's beautiful in here." She spoke when the pop of the cork and its impressive echo around the room came to a stop.

"This was the room that needed the most restoration. I'm very proud of it. It's barely ever used, though, which is a shame, but then when you know how much the flooring cost you do tend to worry about crumbs."

"Oh, thanks for that. I'm definitely not going to be able to eat anything now."

"Don't worry." I laughed. "We do own a vacuum."

I carried over the two champagne flutes, passed one to her then offered mine forward.

"A toast." I looked deep into her eyes. "*Good Manors.*" I lifted my glass and tipped it toward her.

"*Good Manors,*" she echoed and touched her flute to mine.

I watched as she took a sip, the bubbles licking her ruby red lips. I didn't know how long I stared at her but she eventually dropped her gaze and I shook myself out of the stupor.

"Food, that's what we need next." I coughed and walked back over to the side table. "I know we're in a very traditional space but I thought something meze inspired would be good. I don't want to spend half the night in the kitchen." I picked up the silver tray and carried it back to her. I popped little bowls on the table, filled with olives and mini mozzarella, roasted peppers and sun blush tomatoes, then followed them with plates of cured meats.

"Wow, this is a spread." She gasped.

"Well, I wasn't sure what you liked so I got a bit carried away. There's another load yet, hold on."

I took the tray back with me and headed toward the hot box. I was impressed by how warm it had kept the food. I'd borrowed it from the caterer we used for weddings. Well, they'd left it after the last event so I was fairly certain they'd not mind. I'd made many of the dishes for the first time from recipes I'd found online, things like patas bravas and tortilla, and mixed them with my own favorite, paella. I'd never traveled outside the UK but I did enjoy trying foods from exotic locations. It was a way of traveling without leaving the hall.

"Help yourself"—I gestured toward the food then sat down—"there's plenty to go round."

"I don't know where to start." She laughed. "It all looks so good. Thanks, Xander."

"You're welcome, but you've not tried anything yet!"

"It smells wonderful, though, and you didn't poison me last night." She giggled.

"No, that's true." I nodded. "Though I have heard my kisses are deadly."

"Well, I'm still here." She fluttered her lashes and looked down at the end of her fork.

I loved the pink suffusion on her cheeks. Making her blush was fun. I wondered how good her butt cheeks would look in the same shade of pink and had to shift in my seat as my cock leaped in the confines of my trousers.

"So you are. Maybe I didn't kiss you hard enough," I teased.

"I'm not sure if I'm excited or scared. It seems you want to kill me, Xander."

"No, my kiss might slay you but there's a secret potion I know will revive you if that happens."

"Oh, really?"

"Really." I nodded. I think the champagne bubbles had gone straight to my head, or maybe my decision to go for it was making me so brazen.

"Well, in that case then I won't worry anymore."

"Good."

I picked things from plates and bowls but didn't pay any attention to what I was grabbing. Food was really the last thing on my mind. I might have been brave, but I wasn't quite ready to sweep her off her feet and fuck her then and there. I had to work up to that. Or at least I hoped she'd let me work up to that.

"Have you managed to write your article then?" I asked. We had a whole meal to get through. A little inane conversation would stop me coming in my pants before I even got to kiss her, I hoped.

"I've got my notes done now. It'll need tweaking and it might change depending on the images I get in the morning but yeah, it's mostly complete."

"I admire your way with words, India. I wasn't very good at school. Well, Mum homeschooled me mostly. We concentrated on bookkeeping and business studies. I hated reading and writing even back then."

"I always had my nose in a book when I was a kid, still love to read when I can. I think my love of words has come from that."

"I had so much to see and do here I didn't bother with books. I was in with the livestock from being five. I saw a lamb being born about that time but my mum didn't like it when I told her the details so I wasn't allowed to go near the livestock much from then on. But I'd help in the fields and with the machinery. I say help, I probably just got in the way."

"Aw, seems a little sad that you are boxed up in your office these days."

"Well, I still get out as much as possible, but it's just the luck of the draw. I'm the lord of the manor so I have to run it. Well, correction. I'm a poor lord of the manor so I can't afford to employ anyone else to run it for me."

"An important distinction." She nodded. "I admire your determination, you know."

"I'm not sure if it's determination or pure madness." I prodded at an olive on my plate and lifted it to my lips. I wasn't really hungry and the savory fruity smell that normally piqued my appetite definitely did quite the opposite.

"Whatever it is, I admire it." India had her hair up in an intricate bun but one strand of jet black hair with its neon bright tip had come loose at the front. She wrapped it around her finger and tucked it behind her ear. "You've faced many challenges and you keep on going. I know that's not easy." Her face dropped, her eyes had lost their sparkle. I knew she was talking from experience.

I reached across the table and gave her arm a squeeze.

"I've wanted to give up so many times. Mum kept me going when she was alive and her memory keeps me going now but I don't know how long that will work. How much longer I can keep shoveling the shit I really don't know." Why I was so comfortable with her still plagued me. I kept revealing private information to her. Was she manipulating me with her journalistic wiles? I wasn't sure I'd be able to notice it if she was.

"I know why." She took a sip from her champagne flute and sat back in her chair.

The fire crackled and I was suddenly struck by the comforting scent of burning wood, the pine and smoke apparent as I waited for her to tell me why.

"You know that in the end it's all going to be worth it. You can see the success that Mallard's will be."

"I dream about it," I confessed.

"What do you dream?" she whispered, propping her chin in her hands, leaning her elbows on the table.

"I'm walking round the hall, every room restored and gleaming in bright summer sunshine. There's a queue up the driveway of people waiting to get in and I just can't stop smiling."

"That's not a dream, it's a vision."

"I hope so." I sighed. "I keep going because in my darkest hours, I dream that dream. And when I hear bad news or something breaks or I realize there's not a penny left in the coffers, I see those rooms, that queue of people and I find a little grain of strength left deep inside."

"You'll see it for real one day, I'm certain of it."

"Thank you." Silence fell between us. It wasn't uncomfortable but I didn't want it to extend much longer because I worried that's how it would finish up, that the weight of my honesty would quash any budding friendship. I glanced around the room, looking for inspiration.

"Hey, do you want to see something cool?"

"Oh, yes, always!" She sat up straight, her back pulling away from the frame of the chair. "What is it?"

"Follow me"—I picked up the candlestick from the middle of the table—"and I'll show you."

"Okay." She sounded a little hesitant.

I supposed the candle confused her. I held out my hand. "There aren't electric lights where I'm taking you, that's why I've got this. You'll like it, I promise. I'll hold your hand."

She grabbed me, her slim fingers cool and soft as I squeezed them.

"Right, no one really knows when these were built or for what reason." I led her past the fireplace, alongside the imposing table and toward the wall-length tapestry that dominated the room. "There are various theories, though."

At the tapestry I let go of her hand and lifted up the left corner. Once the door behind was revealed, I hooked the material over the hook on the wall, placed there just for that very purpose.

"Oooh, a secret room!" she squealed.

"A series of them in fact, connected by passageways."

"Whoa, it's like something out of *Scooby Doo*!" India gasped and her eyes widened as I pushed open the dark wood panel with the cunningly disguised handle.

"I know, right? I found out about them when I was ten. I stumbled across one of the other doorways and it was like I'd found the entrance to a whole other world."

“Yeah, that’s every kid’s dream.” She was on tiptoe, straining to see what was in the dark behind the door.

“I’ll go in first, take the light source, then you can follow me in. Stay close. It’s pretty safe but the passageways go on for miles and up and down stairs. I don’t want you to get lost or to hurt yourself.”

“I’ll stick close,” she said and followed me in.

The smell took me back to the first time I’d entered the complexity of tunnels. I’d been angry and running away from my dad. I’d kicked out at an empty bookcase in the library in a rage. It had shifted and revealed a door behind it.

I had opened it with trepidation and had been hit with decades of must, damp and hidden secrets. It was a heady combination and the same scent greeted us that night.

“Wow,” she whispered, “this is amazing!”

“Isn’t it?” I agreed. “I’ve spent so many happy hours wandering through here and doing… Well, maybe I’ll tell you about that later.” I laughed and shifted the candelabra to my other hand, reaching out to take hers again.

“The historians can’t decide why these passageways and rooms were built. Some say it was a way of spying. Everyone was paranoid back when this place was built. Others attribute it to being a priest hole but I don’t buy that at all. I don’t think the Mallards have ever been particularly pious. I think they were built as a way for the original Lord Mallard to visit his mistress in secret. There’s whole rooms back here, empty now of course, but they could have been really comfy hidey-holes back in the day.”

“I’m not sure if I think that’s romantic or creepy.”

“Probably both,” I laughed, striding confidently on into the dark. I didn’t need the candlelight. I knew every inch of the hidden passageways and had traversed them many, many times over the years.

"He was married to some young thing, though. All about the money and power. It was well-known they hated each other. It's thought that they both had lovers and even suspected they never had sex with each other. They always slept in different rooms."

"God, that's sad. When I marry, I'm going to do it for love."

"Me too, though Mum tried to get me matched up with so many heiresses it was unreal. Even tried it with a few guys too."

"Really?" India exclaimed. "But you're so obviously not gay."

"I'm not gay, no, but I'm not sure it's that obvious. It wasn't to her. I didn't have much to do with girls. I've always been a bit awkward around them."

"Lord, your mum sounds like a right one. Did she ever give up trying to match-make you?"

"She lost interest in it for a while but then when she was diagnosed with the cancer she had a go at it again. Determined to get me shacked up before she died."

"Sorry." She shook her hair. "That was insensitive of me."

"Nah, it's fine. You're right. She controlled me all through her life, still manages to do it now she's dead. I loved her, though, love her still." The last word caught in my throat and India squeezed my hand.

"Of course, I can see that."

"She set me up on some awful dates, though." I chuckled. "None of which I brought back here."

"Did you ever bring anyone back here?"

"No, never. You're the first."

"Am I?" She smiled. "Aw, thank you."

"You're welcome." I blushed. I'd always kept the tunnels and rooms a secret. I was sure some of the staff knew about them. They'd lived and worked in the place for so long they'd be bound to have stumbled over them, but I'd never actively spoken about them to anyone. Had never thought of showing anyone until India.

"So what did you get up to in here then?" She nudged me with her shoulder. "Tell me."

"Well," I said. "Oh, watch out, we're going down a couple of steps here, yep, that's it." I steadied her, and we stepped down then moved to the right, into a small room.

"This is one of my favorite spots in the whole of the house."

It was simply a small room, a wooden bench along one side, like a shelf built into the wall but at the perfect sitting height. In the opposite corner there was a smaller, triangular shelf fitted into the corner. I put the candle down on that shelf as India squeezed in beside me. It was just big enough for us both to fit in, with a little breathing space.

"Why? It's so small."

"That's why. I felt safe here, still do. I used to keep some of my most treasured possessions here."

"What?"

"Porn mags," I confessed, looking down at the bench and not into her eyes.

"Oh." She giggled. "Now I have a bit of an idea what you got up to in here."

"Yeah." I looked up. "I don't think I need to say any more."

"No." She laughed. "But I think I'd like you to elaborate for me."

"Would you?"

She nodded, keeping her gaze locked with mine.

"I mean, what is there to tell? I was uncomfortable doing that kind of thing in my room. It always felt so public out there. So many people who could disturb me. I mean, folks would knock but cleaners and staff were always in my room and I didn't want anyone to find my stash. Obviously because they contained naked girls and people would work out what I did with them."

She inclined her head ever so slightly, her eyes flickering with something. Lust maybe, or was I just transferring my emotions onto her?

"So the perfect answer was to bring my stash down here. Things might have been found—I wasn't sure I was the only person who knew about the passageways—but it wouldn't be connected to me at all. And this room is so small, the entrance so tiny, I was sure no one would ever discover me even if they did walk past. It's a little cupboard, who would bother looking in here?"

"It couldn't have been comfortable," she purred, looking over to the bench.

"I had a blanket and some cushions on there. Got rid of them years ago because, well, they were here for the duration of my teenage years and never washed. When I realized how disgusting that was I disposed of them. But it was pretty cozy in here back in the day. I could comfortably spend hours on the bench."

"Oh." Her breath hitched and she licked her lips. I wanted to lick them for her.

"I had to be careful not to stay down here too long. I didn't want to arouse suspicion. I made sure the staff were busy, Mum was occupied and Dad was out of the way first, but as soon as the perfect conditions were in place I'd head down here to escape and, erm, let off a bit of steam."

"What were the magazines like? How did you get them?" she asked, shifting weight from one foot to another and stumbling slightly on the uneven floor.

I moved closer, steadying her with my free arm.

"I'm fairly sure they were my father's. I found them in an old filing cabinet in the library. The lock had seized so I took it upon myself to open it. I've always liked to tinker and I was convinced something important was trapped in there. I was surprised to find what I did. Magazines from the seventies, all different titles, all kinds of kink."

"Kink?" She put her hand on my waist.

I wasn't sure if she was trying to steady herself or if she was coming on to me.

"Mm, yes. Everything from women covered in whipped cream to spanking and other stuff that might twist your innocent little mind."

"Innocent?" She laughed. "Yeah, right. Which did you like the most?"

I was very aware of how close we were, where her hand rested.

"The spanking," I replied, and she shuddered against me.

Chapter Eleven

India Grace

I didn't know which was more surprising, the revelation of Mallard's secret passageways or the revelations of Xander Patrick's teenage years. The space we were in was so tight and confining, the candlelight flickered against dark paneling and beyond us it was sheer black. We were cocooned in a secret place, somewhere separate from the real world. Maybe it was somewhere I could let my desires for Xander free.

"Why those ones?" I asked. My voice sounded raspy even to me.

"Because the images of bare-bottomed women fed my own fantasies the most."

I squeaked—the sound slipped from my lips unconsciously and my cheeks blazed with heat moments after.

"Are you okay? Are you scared?" Xander brought his other arm around me, holding me closer, protectively shielding me.

I melted into his arms and pressed my lips to his.

"Not scared." I gasped, pulling apart for breath. "Turned on." I kissed him again and he eagerly responded, lips molded to mine, his hands wandering up and down my back over the deliberately provocative dress I'd chosen to wear and down to my thighs. My skin ached when he touched my flesh, and I arched my back to push more of me against him, pulling my lips from his.

"Thank fuck for that," he said, nibbling along my collarbone between words, "because I am too."

He pushed up my dress and traced along my thighs to the slight lacy knickers beneath. Grasping at the material of his shirt as the coil of desire tightened in the pit of my stomach, I waited for his next move. His lips stilled on my neck and his fingertips grazed the crotch of my knickers. I moaned and he pressed harder, the hesitant touch transformed by urgency.

"So wet." He gasped, looking up at me until I captured his mouth with mine again, and as our tongues dueled, he explored over the stretched barrier of my underwear. Crooning and groaning against his lips, I shook against him. The mounting desire drove all worry from my mind. It was possibly the most stupid thing I'd ever done. The one person in the whole world I shouldn't shag was the man pressed against me, slipping his fingers into my knickers at that very moment. I didn't care, I wanted him.

"I need to fuck you," he growled. "Now."

"Yes, fuck, yes," I mewled, and although his fingers withdrawing from between my thighs was a disappointment at first, when he hooked them into my waistband and yanked them off me I giggled with delight. I pushed him back onto the bench with a bump and a slightly concerning creak of wood. He shook his head at me.

"Naughty girl." He undid his belt, and I became fixated on his hands. The way he eased the buckle apart. "All this would be listed, if they knew about it. You've got to be more respectful of my property."

"Yes, Sir." I bit my lip as he flicked open his fly and unzipped his trousers.

"Come here and respect me," he demanded and hooked his cock outside his pants.

I walked toward him, and he pulled me over to kiss him, encouraging my hips forward until I parted my thighs around him and knelt with knees either side of his, spread open for him, my skirt rucked up around my waist.

"I want you." He groaned. "I really fucking do but I don't have any protection."

"I'm on the pill," I replied, "and I'm, you know, clean."

"I'm sure. I just didn't want to go ahead without asking—are you okay for us to go ahead?"

"Yes"—I nodded—"very much so."

We continued to kiss. I bent my knees and pushed down, meeting his dick while it probed up toward me. I stretched around him, pressing my kiss harder against his lips. I wanted to consume him, make him burn with the lust I did, to pull him into me and keep him there on the brink of ecstasy.

Bucking up and down broke the connection of our lips. I looked down at him and was surprised to find his eyes open too, the shocking blue aimed straight at me. Even in the flickering candlelight I could see his widened pupils. The visual added to the sound of his rasping pants, and the feel of his erection inside me confirmed that he lusted for me just as much as I wanted him.

I couldn't keep my eyes open. I closed them and a shudder of ecstasy ran through me, a breath of cold air tickling the back of my neck. I bent back to press my breasts against him. He tore at my dress. If I wasn't so turned on I'd have been pissed off—it was my very best outfit—but as he ripped and pulled until he revealed bare flesh then took my nipple into his mouth, my protests died before I uttered them.

I was devoured. He nipped and licked and kissed the breast he'd revealed, content to palm and press the other through the velvet of the material. I pressed hard against him at the bottom of each thrust, the shock waves bathing my clit in heat, mini-explosions detonating in my cunt and my mind with each impact.

He tightened his grip on my boob, dug his teeth into my nipple, and I cried out with the pain, which on top of the pleasure was almost too much yet at the same time perfectly right. He throbbed within me as his teeth slackened and a groan bathed my tortured breast in warm, soothing breath. He strained against me and I continued to rock, taking all his orgasm within me and still aching for more.

"Fuck," he groaned. "Fuck, you're too good." He kissed me, and my pussy muscles tightened around him. He gasped into my mouth. "I wanted that to last forever."

"Me too," I whispered back, cupping his face.

"Well, the night is still young and this passage pretty much leads to my bedroom…"

"Lead the way." I winked. "I'm not tired yet."

I scrambled off him. He fastened his trousers, and I popped my breast back within the confines of my bra and dress. I was just going to bend and pick up my knickers when I noticed Xander had them in his hand.

He tucked the scarlet lace into his jacket pocket and winked at me.

"Come on, I'll lead you back to the servants' quarters."

"Was the original Lord's mistress a servant then?" I pondered, Xander pulling me along the brick corridor.

"They don't know but I think probably not. The passageways lead directly into a couple of the bedrooms, the library, dining room and even the basement, but the entrance to the servants' quarters is in a closet. I think that was more a practical measure – it is the only door in the run of the passages that has a lock on it."

"Oh, curious."

"Indeed. Now watch your step, these stairs are uneven and kinda tiny."

He let me go up in front of him. He held the candle high in one hand and gently grasped my waist with the other. I was sheltered by him. We wound up a tight spiral stairway, the old wood creaking and groaning with each step.

"Okay, so we'll take a right here. To the left are the staterooms."

"I have no idea where we are." I laughed. I was completely turned around.

"Not far from my room." He smirked. "Come on."

It didn't take us long to reach a door at the end of a corridor. It was locked with a huge, old-fashioned key.

"This is how I first discovered it. Clearly it was designed so that someone in the passageway could get out but no one else could get in."

He turned the key in the lock and eased the door open.

"That was very quiet," I whispered.

"I keep the hinges well oiled," he replied, also in a whisper. "Mary's room is only a few doors away from here."

We came out in an airing cupboard, the wall lined with shelves stacked up with sheets, towels and blankets. When Xander closed the door, it was hidden by several more shelves. Xander opened the door at the other end of the huge cupboard then beckoned me to follow. We walked along for a few doors. I finally recognized where we were. My room was at the opposite end of the corridor we were heading along.

His room looked not unlike mine. A little bigger, with enough space for a double, or maybe it was a king-size bed, along with a wardrobe and chest of drawers. The walls were the same magnolia—nothing really marked the room as his apart from the scent of him, a deep, grassy musk.

He turned a key in the door lock behind me. I didn't look round. I savored the feeling of being locked in. Locked in with Xander. I felt safe and scared, excited and petrified. My stomach bubbled with lust, anticipation and fear. What was going to happen next?

When Xander pulled me into his embrace, he'd taken off his jacket and loosened his tie.

"Now we're here, what shall we do?" he asked, eyebrow crooked.

"Whatever you want…" The words blurted out but I thought for a moment before uttering the last one. The last one was an invitation to indulge in more than just sex—"Sir."

"Oh God, where do I start?" He swept the rebellious strand of hair back from my face and inspected me. "Are you sure you mean that?"

"Yes." I stared right back at him. "Sir."

"We need to establish limits, then, a word that tells me you're not happy."

"Harriet," I said without hesitation.

"Okay, that'll work." He laughed and kissed me.

I could still feel the mirth on his lips, his smile melting into mine. Xander pulled back abruptly. "I've decided what I want. I want you to strip for me. I need to see you naked." He stepped back and settled himself on the end of his bed.

I was stunned, stiff with fear. *Strip off, just like that?*

"Come on, India, we don't have all night. Don't make me spank you."

Did I want him to spank me? Well, yes, I did, but I also didn't want to disappoint him so early on and I really wanted to have sex again so I kicked off a shoe. It was a start at least.

"Good girl," Xander purred and pulled off his tie.

I shook off my other shoe and took a deep breath. I was a little shaky but I tried not to let my insecurities stop me. I'd not been fully naked in front of a man since Tom and we'd worked up to that over time.

Weirdly, looking directly at Xander helped because I could see the open lust in his eyes. I started by unhooking my necklace. It was the only safe item I had to remove. Well, that and my earrings, which followed.

"Come on, India, don't tease," he growled.

I lifted my dress. One item of clothing and I'd be pretty close to naked. Xander had my knickers so once I lost the dress I'd be naked from the waist down.

Like stripping off a plaster, I started lifting the hem gently then ripped it up and over my head in one fast action before throwing it to the floor. When I looked back toward the bed, Xander was unbuttoning his shirt but he was looking right back at me, not concentrating on what his fingers were doing at all.

It was so embarrassing to be naked and on display. I was aware of every inch of my body. The good bits and the ones I wasn't so friendly with. I closed my eyes as I reached behind me to unbuckle my bra. Shutting my eyes meant I didn't have to look at myself and freak out. I just took off the bra and stood.

He didn't make a noise. Eventually I peeled open an eye to check what was going on. Xander was staring at me. Raking his gaze up and down my body. I squeezed my eyes shut again.

"No need to be so shy, India, you're beautiful. Come here."

It became easier when he commanded me. I moved because he told me to and I wanted to please him, and making him happy, doing what he wanted me to, turned me on. I strode forward, eyes open. I fixed my gaze steadily on a point about an inch above his head.

"Look at me, India."

I tipped my head and met his gaze.

"You are fucking beautiful, absolutely fucking beautiful. I'd stand you in the grand hall for the visitors to admire if I could. You'd get a bit cold, though, and some people just can't keep their hands to themselves."

A flash of an image fluttered before my eyes, like a Polaroid dropping from a camera. Me, naked at the bottom of the grand stairwell. Arms demurely to my sides, thighs closed, head bowed in a classic pose and a hand covering my breast, squeezing it.

"Oh, you like that don't you?" He grabbed my hand and pulled me down until I was level with his lips. "You do, don't you?"

I nodded, cheeks hot, flesh cold except for the hand he was still holding.

"God, if I wasn't turned on it'd be so much fun to play with you, to take you there, make you stand on the cold marble. Maybe leave you there. Watch you from afar. Fuck. I'd have to be the guy who gets handsy with you, though."

He pulled me forward violently, and I stumbled onto him. He fell backward then I bounced on top of him and he laughed.

"Another time. I'll do that another time. Right now I just want to fuck you."

"Oh, please." I gasped, pressing my pelvis down against his. "Please."

"God, the things I could do to you, the things I want to do to you, India."

Xander gripped my face between his hands and kissed me so hard, so passionately, that I forgot to breathe. When he pulled back, I gasped, my lungs bursting, my heart beating with excitement. I needed oxygen but I wanted his kiss more. Reaching forward for another kiss, he caught me off balance, gripped my hips and pushed me over onto my back. I squealed as I came to rest on the very edge of the mattress. An inch farther over and I'd have fallen off.

"That was close." He nuzzled into my neck, kissed along my jaw line then down into the dip between my collarbone and throat. I grasped at his sides, holding on for dear life as his clothed body pushed down against my skin.

"I'm completely spoilt for choice, India. I don't know what to do next."

Do me! I screamed the words in my head but I didn't let them escape because if Xander had dominant tendencies I knew that would then be the last thing he'd do. Dominant equaled awkward fucker. Intriguing, sexy, hot as hell but bloody awkward all the same.

"Lift your arms, India, lift them over your head."

I stretched up.

"Link them together, that's it."

He kissed lower, across my chest and breasts, licking and teasing my nipples. Even lower he journeyed, over my stomach, the zigzag of stretch marks somehow escaping his notice but he did pause to dip his tongue in my belly button, provoking a snort of laughter from me.

"Keep your hands up there," he commanded before kissing lower. "Don't move them."

I managed it for quite a while. Even when he used his fingers to spread my lips and I felt his breath on my clit, I didn't move. I kept still at his first, tentative lick. Then he was eating me with such enthusiasm that I felt like I was going to rip in two so I dropped my hands down from the position above my head to cradle his.

"Oh, no, no, no. What did I tell you?" He stopped licking, and I realized what I'd done.

Oh shit. "Sorry, Sir." I gasped and raised my hands once more.

"Nope, it's too late now." He scrambled up to his knees and off the end of the bed. "Roll over onto your stomach. I'm going to have to punish you."

"But—"

"But me no buts, young lady," he barked, sending shock waves of lust straight to my cunt. "On your front now, arse up."

I wanted to utter another 'but', to protest. To tell him he was too good and I couldn't help myself, but I knew it'd be hopeless. I would have to take my punishment like a good girl.

"Jesus," he cursed. "What a perfectly spankable arse." He gently stroked over my buttocks, covering me with the whole of his hand, not just his fingertips.

A tumult of emotion raged within me—I wanted him to strike me but I was scared too. I wanted him to continue to stroke and soothe but I also didn't want to miss out on the spanks. Talk about contradictory.

When Xander pulled his hand away from me I tensed up, expecting a strike…but it never came. I wondered what was going on. Imagined I could feel his gaze resting on my buttocks, that he was visually devouring me. I wished he would continue to physically devour me too. While I pondered what I wanted him to do to me the strike came.

The first slaps were relatively gentle and provoked a light *oh* of surprise to fall from my lips. With each impact he hit harder until I was squirming and yelping in pain. My buttocks stung even when his hand wasn't against my flesh and exploded with heat when it was. The constant throb sank through me and seated around my clit. Each new impact shook me with orgasmic vibrations.

"Oh, I think someone's enjoying her punishment." Xander laughed huskily and ran his hand over my sore buttocks, dipped between my cheeks then down into the wetness of my pussy. "Oh, really, really enjoying her punishment." He fucked me with his fingers then. He had one hand on my arse, the pressure intensified by the prickling heat lingering from my spanking. I felt the outline of his digits, the heat of his palm painted on my flesh with pain. The stinging of his steadying hand intensified the pleasure that came from the plunging digits of his other hand, which pumped into me with such precision and power that I lost count of how many times I came over his digits. It blended into a rollercoaster of peaks and troughs, no rest, no break, constant pain and pleasure pummeling my body.

"I've got to have you," he groaned, lifting my hips higher and kneeling on the bed behind me.

The emptiness haunted me. I pushed back, desperate to be filled once more, and he didn't disappoint. He pushed into me quickly, and I eagerly accepted him. His moan of appreciation made me smile with pride. It made my heart swell to know I was pleasing him, I hoped as much as he pleased me.

Xander dug his nails into my hips and dragged me back onto his cock repeatedly. The only noise was the slight groaning of the bed and the slapping sound of our bodies impacting wetly together, punctured with the gasps, moans and pants of pleasure as we both headed toward climax.

The pace intensified, the pressure grew and he tensed inside me. He held still for a moment then slammed into me again. He repeated the rhythm a few times then rubbed my back and slid away from me. I collapsed onto my stomach with a sigh.

Warmth and spice enveloped me as Xander pressed his body against mine. I rolled to face him and snuggled into his embrace, my head resting on his shoulder. He wrapped an arm around my back. I trailed my fingers down the center of his chest, teasing the dark hairs, and enjoyed the warmth and the undulation of his breath.

He stroked my back with a light pressure of swirls and circles, making me tingle and shudder. The touch made me long for more connection with him, reminded me I still needed to come.

I brazenly hooked my thigh over his, opening myself, offering myself, begging for the release I needed. He stilled the hand at my back and traced his other gently along my side, and at the point where my thigh kinked he didn't follow the outer sweep but dipped his fingers down between our bodies. When he touched my swollen lips, I gasped and he pushed forward then slid his digits into my warm wetness. I moaned against the curve of his neck, finishing with a gentle, encouraging kiss against his throat.

It turned me on to hear how wet I was, knowing that some of that wetness was his cum. I shuddered, his fingers embedded inside me.

"God, you're so sexy," he purred.

I opened my eyes and cricked back my neck to look deep into his bright blue eyes. He continued to finger-fuck me. Lust and curiosity shone through his gaze as he intently watched my reactions to his movements. Did he notice the way my eyes widened and how my lips dropped open into an 'o' as the pleasure within me escaped as a groan?

I watched him watching me, him licking his lips and swallowing. His face tensed with arousal, his eyes, his deep, penetrating eyes overflowing with erotic energy, and eventually the pleasure of watching became too much and my lids closed once more. Xander's lips imprinted onto mine, and I groaned my arousal into his mouth. The louder I got, the more passionately he kissed me. He pulled his fingers from inside me and changed his motion to rubbing against my clit, making me whimper and pant all the more.

We continued to kiss. I felt like I melted into him, my toes pointing back and resting on the back of his calf. I tensed and shook with the first vibrations of my orgasm. I clung to him, nails digging into his chest. I was washed over with lust, my whole body shaking from the impact of ecstasy. I gripped onto him and he stroked my back with tenderness as he swept his other fingers gently down over my wet lips. I trembled and snapped my thighs closed, trapping his hand between my legs.

"Gotcha."

"Uh-huh," he responded. "I like it."

"Me too." I panted and curled up against his chest. Unbidden tears mounted behind my eyes. I squeezed them closed. I couldn't cry. I glimpsed for a moment how good we could be together, and in the next realized it could never happen. I couldn't let it happen.

Chapter Twelve

Xander Patrick

I didn't think India realized that I knew she was crying but I felt her hot tears on my chest. I just held her. Why she was crying was a mystery to me but I wanted to comfort her anyway. After all, I had just experienced the most intensely pleasurable fuck of my life.

Okay, there hadn't been many, but even those few kinky interludes I'd shared with Ariana didn't compare to the intensity of emotion and the amazing reactions of India. What a woman, what a sensual creature. She gave herself up so freely to me. My heart sank—she would leave Mallard's in the morning.

I stroked her hair and kissed her forehead. I couldn't tell her that I wanted her to stay, couldn't confess she was the best sex I'd ever had and I'd really like to have some more. She'd think I was a total freak. A woman like India Grace wouldn't fall in love at first fuck. I was starting to suspect that maybe I had.

The longer the silence lasted, the harder it was to break.

"Can we move under the covers? It's cold." India's words broke through the heavy atmosphere.

"Sure, sure."

We shuffled and rearranged and ended up below my duvet, still huddled close.

"You can sleep here tonight if you want," I said, hoping I sounded casual. "Share body heat."

"I'd love to but I think I need to go back to my room eventually. Won't look good if someone sees me creeping out of your room in the morning. I don't fuck folks I'm reviewing as a general rule."

"Does that make me special?" I tipped her chin up and made her meet my gaze.

"Yes, it does," India replied.

I kissed her and saw something brewing in the depths of her eyes and I didn't want to see it anymore. A hint of sadness, of regret, which just didn't bode well for me.

"Oh good, do I get extra marks now?" I tried to keep the tone light.

"No, I think I have the marks." She winced dramatically then giggled. "This doesn't count toward the review, no. I don't think all members of the public get this attention as part of their experience of Mallard's, do they?"

"No." I shook my head. "I'd be exhausted if they did."

She chuckled again, her light laugh vibrating through my chest. It felt like my heart was squeezed. God, why was she leaving me so soon?

"I best go." She yawned. "Before I fall asleep."

"Well, if you're sure."

"Yeah, yeah, I am." She sounded like she was trying to convince herself.

She threw back the duvet and danced to the end of the bed to find her clothes.

"Brr, it's cold tonight."

"Then stay in my bed."

"Xander." Something in the tone of her voice, a hitch, a stutter, made me realize I shouldn't push her any further. "I'm sorry but I can't."

"Okay, sorry." I gulped. "Goodnight, India."

"Goodnight, Xander." She pulled on her dress and slipped into her shoes. She carried everything else in her hands.

"See you in the morning?" It was a question but also a statement. I'd make sure I saw her before she left.

"Sure, yeah."

She blew me a kiss on her way out of the door. I pretended to catch it, how suave, then she shut the door and I collapsed back onto my pillows.

I berated myself. How could I be so confident and in control one moment then completely at a loss the next? When we'd had sex it all seemed so right. I'd happily taken control—God, I could have spanked her arse for weeks. Such a beauty, such a wanton beauty. She'd loved it too. She'd truly loved it, and that was the real turn-on.

Why didn't I simply command her to stay in my bed?

Because I knew she'd leave. I had to let her go. And for once it wasn't the voice of my dead mother nagging me about sleeping, quite literally, with the enemy, but the thread of common sense I actually housed in my head.

India Grace was out of my league. I was nothing more than a handy shag for her. She would go back to her city life, her journalistic ways, and forget all about me and Mallard's. She didn't feel any connection to me past whatever sexual chemistry we shared.

I was the only one feeling anything deeper. I was the stupid prat falling for a woman I couldn't have. Talk about history repeating. King of unrequited love, I'd mooned over many women from afar right from my teenage years. I'd rarely asked any of them out. Those I had had nearly always denied me, with the odd exception.

I seemed incapable of love that didn't involve some kind of barrier, some kind of distance that would keep the woman away from me. I craved love intensely yet I was scared of it.

I rolled over and closed my eyes tightly. I had to sleep. I could beat myself up once India left. I had to hold it together until then at least.

* * * *

I slept fitfully that night and had to drag myself out of bed in the morning to check on Harriet and baby. I'd just stepped out onto the dew soaked driveway when Mary yelled my name. I knew it was her—only she could compress my name so sharply.

"Xander!"

I looked round and she wasn't far behind me, shuffling in determined fashion. I waited for her to catch up.

"I've been calling you all down the main stairway."

"Sorry, Mary, I didn't sleep so well last night."

"Well, no, neither did I." She sighed. "I've been looking deeper into the accounts and there's stuff that doesn't add up. I think we're losing livestock."

"How the hell are we doing that?"

"I don't really know but there are more animals being born than we're slaughtering. Now if that were the case we'd be knee-deep in livestock but we're not."

"No, we're not. How many are we out by?"

"I've calculated about a dozen." She sighed. "In the last six months."

I wanted to curse but Mary wouldn't approve. I shook my head violently instead.

"How on earth can that be? Is Phil fiddling us?"

"No." Mary's voice lifted an octave. "I mean no. Phil's been here for almost as long as I have. I can't believe he'd be involved in anything dodgy."

"I know, Mary, but he has direct contact with the slaughterhouse and he's the man who does our butchery. He might be slipping food out with him at the end of the day."

"I'll keep my eye on him." She sighed heavily.

"I will too." I squeezed the top of Mary's arm and smiled. "We'll get to the bottom of it, Mary, I know we will."

"Thank you." She covered my hand with hers. "We will, I know we will. But it's wearying being this untrusting."

"I know what you mean, I really do."

It was difficult being friendly with staff when stuff like this happened. How could I even start to imagine that any of the manor workers would do anything so underhand? I'd known many of them for years—even the newer members haven't been strangers to me. Mum had always said it was best to recruit from those already within our social circle. That connection made the employee more honest because they knew you as a person, not just as a faceless business.

Sure, there were staff members I wasn't fond of. Phil was good at his job but bored me to tears within seconds of starting a conversation. Graham was pretty much every 'ist' in the book but he pretty much hated everyone equally. He wasn't great at being social but the man was fucking brilliant with flowers and bushes, not to mention fixing fences, rebuilding barns and renovating pieces of old farm machinery that went out of fashion in the 60s. That man could get anything to work. I'd have sworn he had some kind of magic in that toolbox of his.

And Gerald had something about him that creeped me out but he loved Mallard's so much he wouldn't do anything to put it in jeopardy. He lived for the place. That left Harry and Jenny, the newbies, and really I wanted to put them in the beyond-thought category. How could such sweet and, to be blunt, thick people even come up with a plot that would confound me and the rest of the staff?

Visiting Harriet and the little one gave me a moment of escape in a dark day. I tried to think of a name for the baby but whenever I thought of girl names they all seemed to lead to India. I sighed, put down fresh hay and headed back to the manor. I didn't want to say goodbye to her but I couldn't bear not to either. I was sick to death of the contradictions but I couldn't do anything about them.

Back at the hall, I found India at the bottom of the main stairs. The marble echoed with the tinkle of her laughter and two other joyful voices that I didn't recognize. A deep baritone chuckle coming from behind Harry's droopy fringe and a light giggle from Jenny, who really didn't look like the kind of woman to giggle at all, let alone lightly.

India had the couple standing behind one another on the stairwell. Both were in their work skivvies, probably just come in from feeding the pigs from the smell of them.

"Come on, really pretend this place belongs to you. Stiffen your backs and your upper lips, lift your noses. No, Jenny, don't snort through your nose."

All the time India talked she stared down the camera lens and clicked. She might be acting like she was trying to get a pose from the pair but she was clicking away as they shook with laughter. I watched the trio—not one of them had noticed me coming in. I lurked in the entrance, hidden behind the second set of doors.

"You're not very good at this, are you?" India sighed. "You're supposed to be serious."

"Sorry, India. He keeps blowing in my ear." Jenny squealed and ducked. "And it tickles."

"Harry, will you behave!" She exclaimed, still clicking away with the camera.

"I'm just breathing, India. I've got to breathe, don't I?"

"You're bloody not just breathing," Jenny cursed. "You're doing it on purpose."

"No I'm not." Harry stuck his tongue out...directly into Jenny's ear.

She yelped, spun and slapped him. The echo bounced off the walls, making it sound much harder than it was.

"Right, you've had it now." Harry grasped Jenny and blew a raspberry on the side of her neck.

"Be careful," India yelled, but there was a lightness to her caution. "We don't want you to fall down those stairs, you might leave a pool of blood and that wouldn't go down well with the tourists."

Jenny wriggled out of Harry's grasp and careened down the stairs. He was in close pursuit, and as he reached the ground he grabbed the back of her overalls and dragged her back to him. She protested and wriggled, but I'd obviously underestimated the kid's strength because he twisted, turned and pulled Jenny into his arms. Not an easy feat. Although by the way Jenny returned his passionate kiss I didn't think she was trying very hard to get away from him.

India cleared her throat, once, twice, then very loudly indeed.

"Oh, forgot you were there." Jenny squirmed. "Erm, have you got any good photos for the article, like?"

"Yeah, loads," she replied. "Have you got an email address? I can send them to you to check over for me before I use them."

I had to smile when Jenny peered at her with such derision.

"No? Okay, I'll print out the best and post them to you."

Jenny nodded. "Great. Thanks, India."

"No, thank you, I got some great shots then."

"India, look what happens when I do this." Harry dug his fingers into Jenny's ribs, and she squirmed, screamed and tore herself away.

As Harry chased her toward me I realized that I was very soon going to be discovered and ducked back behind the door. Before they reached me, Jenny turned and headed in the opposite direction down the corridor. I should have shouted at them for mucking about in the public area of the hall but their sweet, youthful enthusiasm was so palpable I couldn't stop smiling long enough to do it. Once their cries had dissipated, I peeked around the door to be greeted by the lens of India's camera.

"Oh, Xander." She dropped the camera. "I didn't know you were there, I was taking photos of the doors."

"Did you get me?"

"Yeah, I think I did." She looked down at her viewfinder, and I strode toward her. "Yes, yes I did."

I walked up and stood beside her, glanced over her shoulder at the image.

In it I could see the impressive frame of the ancient oak doors, and there I was, just coming into view but with a very obvious grin.

"It's an amazing photo," she said. "The light is fantastic and you look so content. That would make a brilliant lead photo for the article..." She left her sentence hanging.

"I don't know, India. The photo is impressive, you have great skill, but I'm not sure—"

"Please, Xander? That is the most perfect photo. I promise you that it'll do nothing but good for Mallard's if I use it. It really captures something special about you and your relationship to Mallard's."

I sighed. I didn't know if what she said was true but I could hear the real passion in her voice and I just didn't want to deny her.

"Okay, you can use it."

"Really?" she squeaked and turned to stare at me.

"Yes, really." I couldn't go back on it now. Mum turned in her grave, but my heart skipped a beat when she laughed and threw an arm around me.

"Oh, thank you, Xander, you won't regret it."

I held her. I wanted to kiss her, to keep her with me forever, but I knew that wasn't an option. India pulled back from me a moment later, cheeks flushed scarlet. She took a deep breath and spoke. "Thanks, that's great. And thanks for letting me visit. I have to get going now, though."

"Don't be a stranger," I replied with what I hoped was a light smile.

"I'll be in touch soon with the article." Her words sounded awkward, like she was filling the silence.

"Brilliant, looking forward to it." I glanced down at my toes. What more could I say? I knew it was likely the last time I'd ever see her but what could I do to stop it?

"Bye then." She headed toward the impressive staircase. "I'm okay to go up this way, aren't I?"

"Sure." I checked the watch on my wrist. "The visitors won't be allowed in for a good hour and a half yet."

"Okay. Well, bye, Xander."

"Bye, India."

I watched her run up the first few stairs. She turned, looked and opened her mouth. She then closed her sensual lips together, waved and continued up the stairs. I walked away. I couldn't watch her any longer. I couldn't watch my happiness disappear.

Chapter Thirteen

India Grace

I sat on the end of the tiny single bed and stared down at the image of Xander in the viewfinder. His smile was light, natural, and captured a joy that made my heart swell. At the same time tears welled up and before I knew it a shower of them fell onto the picture, obscuring his face. It was stupid. I dashed the tears from my eyes with the back of my hand then wiped them from the screen with the cuff of my jumper.

I switched the camera off and put it back in the case. I had to go. I had to leave Mallard's and Xander Patrick behind me. I would do my utmost to write the most attractive article ever to double and triple their turnover but then that would have to be it.

Fucking Xander had been a mistake. I shouldn't have let my lust control me. He might not be Mallard in name but he was in lineage, and how could I ever have any serious relationship with him knowing what I'd done to his father? How could I keep that from him?

I slung the camera in its case over my shoulder and picked up my suitcase. It was time to go. More tears threatened to spill over but I couldn't let them. I took a deep breath then walked out of Mallard Hall forever.

Or so I'd thought. An hour later but only a quarter of a mile down the road I began to think differently. I tuned into the local radio station and after an assortment of strange jingles and adverts the travel update was announced.

"There is an overturned lorry on the High Road in Madupton that's blocked both sides of the road. The traffic is backed up both ways and isn't likely to ease any time soon. Motorists are advised to avoid the area."

I switched off the radio and looked in my rear mirror. The car behind wasn't too close and I had room in front of me so in a rush of rash adrenaline I made a U-turn and headed right back to Mallard's. The traffic was easy, I made it back in a matter of minutes and once I parked up I headed for the shop.

"What are you doing here?" Mary asked when I popped my head round the door. I knew she'd be there.

"There's an upturned lorry on the road out of here, the traffic is trailing back both ways. So I turned round. Am I okay to stay here until it's sorted?"

"Oh, I'm sure you are. Xander's in the office, though, and you better check with him. He is the actual boss, you know."

"So they say," I laughed. "Thanks, Mary."

"You're welcome, dearie." She waved as I headed across to the hall. Spring sunshine bathed the light hall in a golden glow. I marveled at the richness of the ancient stone and tried really hard to think about extra information I could gather for my article. Not Xander Patrick.

He was leaning over his desk when I got there, scrutinizing a piece of paper in minute detail.

"What is it, Mary?" he asked, without looking up.

"It's not Mary," I replied, and his head snapped up. "It's me, India."

"India?" His intonation rose, his surprise showing.

"Yep, I couldn't stay away." I giggled nervously. "There's been an accident on the main road. The traffic's backing up for miles. Can I stay here until it passes?"

"Yes, of course, of course."

"I'm sure I can find something to keep me occupied, I'll get some extra info for the article. Maybe I can—"

"I'll show you round."

"Oh, no, you don't have to, I know you're busy."

"No, no, I insist." He pushed the papers on his desk into a hurried pile then pulled open the drawer in the desk and stuffed the papers in there. "Let me show you. I want to."

"Well, if you're sure." I wanted to spend the day with him more than anything else, even if my conscience was screaming at me to run away.

"I'm sure," he answered, brooking no nonsense.

Xander strode off, and I meekly followed behind him. I wanted to reach out and grab his hand, to hold it and tell him I didn't want to go. I wanted more of him. There was even a part of me that wanted to tell him my secret—the burden of it hurt my heart.

But I couldn't hold his hand, I couldn't tell him the truth. One might ruin the magazine and its reputation—I couldn't have people thinking I rated a place on the shagability of the owner—and the other would break Xander's heart, and I couldn't do that. I'd already hurt him before I'd ever met him. I couldn't bear to inflict any more pain on him.

So I followed him. Fate or coincidence or God—whatever or whoever it was that had brought me back to him had given us the opportunity to spend some more time together. I'd use that opportunity to give Xander everything that I could. To give him all of me for a few hours. To show him how sorry I was for the past even if I couldn't express that to him in words.

He led me back down the corridor and toward the main stairway and the visitor end of the manor.

"If Gerald was in the Grand Hall before"—Xander looked at his watch—"he should have visited where I want to take you already."

Just on the other side of the main stairway, he ducked into one of the doors and I followed him. He shut the door behind us, pulled a bunch of keys from his inside pocket and turned an ancient key in the old brass lock.

"Just in case the tourists are still about." Xander smiled.

"This is stunning." I remembered the room from my tour with Gerald. The grand bathroom. It was just like it used to be, old-fashioned bath in the middle of the room. When the house had been built there hadn't been running water and the Mallards had preserved this one bathroom in all its ancient glory.

A stand in the corner held a massive porcelain basin and jug, decorated with a delicate floral pattern. In another corner lay a couple of the huge copper jugs the servants would have filled up with hot water from the kitchens and lugged up to the bathroom to fill the impressive bath every time one of the family wanted one.

"We didn't have to do much with this room, it's always been like this."

"Really?"

"Yeah, this posh end of the house has never really been used much." Xander shrugged.

"So you've never had a bath in there then?" I giggled.

"No." He shook his head, the dark locks bouncing. "I never have."

"I'd love to bathe in there."

"Oh yes?"

"Yeah, have a hot, hunky man pour hot, bubbly water all over me as I stretch out and relax? I could go for that." I turned to him and wrapped my arms around his neck. There was no need to be coy and I wanted him to know the hot guy I mentioned was him.

"Now if the kitchen wasn't so far away and the house full of strangers I'd be willing to help you out with that fantasy. You'll have to store it up for another time."

My heart sank—there would never be another time. I didn't dwell on it, though, as our lips met and I was consumed by his closeness, his caress.

"I might not be able to bathe you, my love, but I would like to get you naked."

Xander pushed his hands up under my top and lifted it over my head. I was happy to let him strip me—I was ready for whatever would come from that. He threw the light, floral material onto the floor and put his hands on my waist again.

He studied me. The harder he looked, the hotter my cheeks felt. After a moment that stretched on forever, he shifted his hands and moved them up my back until he hit the band of my bra then he unfastened the clip, after only one false start. He peeled the cotton away from my body.

I held my breath. My breasts dipped to rest in their natural position. Mine weren't the perky boobs of a fake porn star. For a moment I worried about that, then Xander cupped them tenderly in his hands, moaned, and all worry—hell, all thought—left my mind. Softly he flicked his thumbs back and forth, brushing over my nipples. They puckered and tightened with every flick. My breathing deepened, each breath an aroused pant.

"Not quite naked yet," he mumbled, looking up and smiling at me. He then looked down again and pushed my skirt off my hips.

"Kick off your shoes," he demanded.

I obeyed, dislodging my skirt at the same time. I was completely naked and he hadn't even taken off his jacket. I shuddered, not from cold but from the realization that he had stripped me for his pleasure. I was vulnerable and naked at his command. He could ask me to do anything. And I knew I would do it without much hesitation. Whatever he wanted, I wanted.

Xander glanced round the room, his gaze calculating. I watched him intently, and suddenly his face lit up with a smile.

"Stand over there, by the jugs." He pointed, and I walked.

Very aware that he was looking at me, I took my time and accentuated my hip movements. I'd give him something seriously sensual to appreciate. When I reached the wall, I stopped, facing it.

"This is an amazing view, India, but please turn around and face me."

I turned around, and he nodded.

"This view is just as pleasant." He smirked and walked toward me. "You're very beautiful."

"Thank you, Sir." I dipped my head, cowed slightly by the compliment.

"You're welcome, now look at me."

I lifted my chin and looked at Xander again. He stopped just a step in front of me. "Spread your legs."

I followed his instructions, widening my stance. He smiled and stepped away from me.

I squinted and crinkled my brow in confusion. Where was he going?

"Now, you would like me to treat you, pour hot water over you in that tub, you'd probably expect me to scrub you down too, right?"

"I would like that, Sir," I answered, carefully weighing up my answer.

"Yes, I would too," Xander agreed. "But for such a treat, India, you need to earn it, well, urn it, in fact." He laughed as he picked up two of the giant jugs and carried them back to me.

"Extend your arms."

I lifted them out from my body.

"Straighten them."

I pushed them higher.

"Perfect." He put the handle of one jug into my left hand, and I closed my fist around it. "Keep it there, don't let it fall."

It was heavy. Not World's Strongest Man heavy but it already strained my muscles to hold it up like that. Moments later, he put the other jug into my right hand. I gripped it and he let the weight fall.

"Okay, I don't want to see them drop at all, not even an inch. If you lower either one of them I will stop what I'm doing immediately. Do you understand?"

"Yes, Sir," I replied quickly. I didn't want to delay proceedings any further. Even if I didn't know what he was going to do to me.

"Good." He stepped closer to me, reached a hand round my body and squeezed my bum, which was still stinging somewhat from our earlier interaction. I hissed but kept the jugs in pretty much the same position. A moment later, his other hand pressed against my pubis.

His clothing grazed my skin as his fingers sank down through my pubic curls to the top of my slit.

He tapped his pointer there. I wanted to squirm, to stand on tiptoes and make his fingers contact my clit like I needed them to but I waited patiently, arms aching from wrist to shoulder. The damn jugs weighed a ton, maybe not literally but it felt like it.

Each second felt like a millennium but eventually he inched his fingers lower and pressed against my clit. I shuddered. Xander paused and the jugs clattered but I didn't drop them. He continued to press lower until his fingers dipped inside me. I moaned at his filling me and he pumped into me a couple of times, watching my right arm intently. I held the handles tight and prayed for the strength to keep on holding the weights out.

He didn't continue with the same action for long, he ran the moisture of my wet pussy up my slit and swirled it around my clit.

"Fuck." I gasped. My arms ached, my clit throbbed and my legs wobbled.

Xander laughed. Wicked man. He didn't stop rubbing, and soon I could feel my orgasm building. I wasn't thinking about my arms anymore, all my attention was centered on my clit. Then he stopped, and I realized my arms had dropped a little. I straightened them back up.

"Good girl. For that recovery, I'll be lenient." He continued his stroking action, three fingers up and down between my wet lips, rolling up and over my clit then down again in a pleasurable rhythm. I held myself as stiffly as I could, my whole body straining to keep my arms up. Beads of sweat pricked at my skin. I knew my face had gotten redder. The heat of exertion warmed past my cheeks to my lip, forehead and beyond.

Each strumming move of his fingers elicited a new noise from between my lips. Pants, groans, moans and curses pushed out of my mouth as I tried, oh how I tried to keep those jugs raised.

I felt Xander's head dip—he had it rested against my shoulder. He was looking down my body, not at my arms, so I relaxed them ever so slightly, hoping he was distracted by what he was viewing. Maybe a little respite might mean I'd be able to let go and come all over his hands.

But he clearly felt the shift and stopped what he was doing immediately.

"Oh, India. You'd been doing so well."

"Sorry, Sir." I slumped. I couldn't hold up the weights anymore, I just couldn't.

"You tried your hardest, but you do know that means you don't get to come."

"Yes, Sir."

Xander stepped away from me.

"Put the jugs down, India."

I was bitterly disappointed with myself. I'd let Xander down and that hurt me.

"Oh, don't look so sad," he comforted. "You did very well and I was being decidedly mean."

I stood up, and he wrapped me up in a hug and I squeezed him tightly in return.

"I did try." I gasped. Tears pricked behind my eyes but I wouldn't let them fall.

"I know you did, I'm proud of you." Xander kissed my forehead, and I pressed myself closer to him, inhaled his warming musk and stemmed the flow of the stupid tears. Disappointing Xander had hurt me. I didn't want to do it again.

He tipped back my head, smiled at me and kissed my lips. I kissed back, throwing all my dedication, all my eagerness to please into that kiss.

"God, you're so fucking hot, India," Xander whispered. "But you better get dressed. Gerald will be round with the next tour soon. We need to get out of here to a new room. I know where we can go too, where we definitely won't be disturbed."

My heart jumped in my chest. That sounded promising.

Chapter Fourteen

Xander Patrick

I didn't know where that mean idea had leaped from but seeing India strain to hold those two weights up while I'd pleasured her pleased me beyond measure. I'd nearly let her get away with the slip, just so I could watch her come, feel her contract on my fingers and hear her cries of delight, but rules were rules and she had broken them.

The poor girl looked completely mortified, I didn't want her upset by the game so I held her and told her how proud I was. I would have happily stayed and played longer but I was aware of the time and the last thing I wanted was Gerald trying to get in with a group of nosy old tourists.

She dressed quickly. The movement of her breasts and thighs as she wiggled into clothing took my breath away. It was just as arousing as if she were taking things off.

"Don't bother with the bra." I picked it up and stuffed it in my jacket pocket. "You won't need it."

"Yes, Sir," she answered, clearly shaken by my confiscation of her underwear.

"I'll enjoy watching your tits bounce for me," I said with a wink.

"Good," she replied with a sigh. "I'm glad, Sir."

She slipped her top on and while she put the second shoe back on her foot I went to the door and unlocked it. I peeked out into the corridor—all was quiet.

"Come on." I beckoned to her. "Follow me."

I didn't turn round—I knew she'd be in pursuit. There were few places in the whole manor where I was thoroughly secure in the knowledge that no one else would go there. The secret passages were one, but there was nowhere really comfortable to fuck there and we'd done that already. I had one more ace up my sleeve and no one else ever went there. Mostly because I told them they couldn't, that it was unsafe.

I led India into the servants' end of the home. It was weird to think of it as that. It'd always been referred to that way, but really, it was where I'd grown up and lived. The lord of the manor who slept in the servants' quarters. I was more of a servant than a lord—the place kept me enslaved. Not that I minded—it was my life, my soul. I couldn't begin to imagine what I would be without it.

At the very back of the servants' quarters there was an old, wobbly set of stairs. At the bottom hung a 'beware' sign. I walked past it and glanced over at India, who was hovering near the bottom step.

"It's okay, it's safe, trust me."

She nodded and followed me up the creaking steps. I pulled out my bundle of keys from my pocket, flicking her knickers out with them. I pushed the flimsy material back into my pocket with a smile then opened the attic door, pausing to pick up the huge torch I leave just inside the doorway.

"No lighting up here," I explained. "So watch your step."

Flicking on the torch, I revealed the majesty of this huge, open space. It covered the length of the servants' quarters, with plaster inserts here and there breaking it up into several rooms. The attic we stood in was around twenty feet in length and virtually the same width. High beams and low ones, old and solid.

"Wow, Xander, this is amazing!" India gasped. "How far does this stretch?"

"See the door there?" I pointed the beam of light to the far left corner.

"Yes, I see it."

"Well that leads on to another section like this and there's another one after that. I've seen it on the blueprints but the doorway there into the next section is blocked up. I can't push past whatever is behind the door. One day I want to break open the seal, to see what's beyond it, but I need to have money in place to do it. I don't know what will greet me at all."

"God, that's exciting. If you do it, let the mag know, they'd love a scoop like that… The hidden attic of Mallard Hall, unveiling the secrets of centuries past."

"Nice, you do have a way with words."

"Thank you, that's why I'm a journalist." She winked.

"Well, if it gets the famous India Grace back to Mallard's, I'll certainly think seriously about it."

She blushed and stared down at her toes. I couldn't believe such a beautiful, vivacious woman was so shy.

"So, why's there a warning sign down there?"

"Because I don't know what's past the door. It could be dangerous back there but in here, it's perfectly fine."

"Another one of your escapes?" she asked, her eyes pulled to the blanket and cushions to the side of us and the pile of books and magazines.

"Yeah, this room has special memories for me." I smiled. "I like to revisit from time to time."

"What kind of memories?" she asked me, her head tipped to the side thoughtfully.

"I'll tell you. Let's sit down first and get comfortable."

I walked over to the blanket and sat down then made room for her to sit beside me. India followed suit, and I scooched a little closer. I needed to feel her close to me.

"Okay, are you comfy?"

She shuffled in place, and I put an arm around her shoulders. She didn't tighten up—in fact she moved closer to me. I knew we'd fucked but there seemed to be something deeper, more intimate, in our cuddling together.

"Yes, comfy now."

"Okay, then I shall begin." I let my arm slip down her back and settle behind her, propping myself up and just touching her.

"I was seventeen when Mum employed Ariana. She wasn't known to us before she started, unusual for Mallard's. She worked all over the manor. We didn't have the shop back then but she helped with tours and the livestock as well as cleaning and some admin duties. I saw her all the time.

"She was older than me. It seemed like a huge rift at the time but really seven years isn't that much. At that age, though, I didn't have many years behind me so it seemed like half a life's difference."

India lay her head on my shoulder, and I stopped for a moment and smiled before continuing.

"I was completely transfixed by her. Tongue-tied and awkward. I barely spoke to her for the first nine months she was with us. I just fantasized about it. She'd smile at me occasionally, we'd even manage the odd work-related conversation but that was it."

I took a break, gulped then continued, "Mum must have known I was besotted, well, that's the kind of thing they notice, isn't it?"

India nodded against my shoulder.

"She must have told me a million times several really good reasons why you shouldn't get involved with someone you're employing. I knew exactly who she referred to and actually, her plan totally backfired. It was her impassioned calls to not be involved with a staff member that made me think more and more about it, and eventually I was brave enough to do something about it.

"I started small with 'hellos' and 'how are yous' and moved on to complimenting her at every opportunity I could. Once I took that step the rest was relatively easy. From an acquaintance grew a friendship and from there a flirty seduction. It didn't go like I expected it to, with her taking the lead. I found a voice deep within me, a confidence and swagger, I suppose. I seduced her."

"I can believe it." India smiled up at me, and I leaned down to press a gentle kiss to her lips.

"It surprised me, honestly, scared me a little but I just went with it. I can still remember the first time I kissed her in such detail. I saw her nipping into the airing cupboard and took the opportunity to follow her in. I blocked the door and said hello. She berated me for scaring her and said she had to get on. I told her she wasn't getting past until she kissed me. I was very surprised when she relented without even a moment's protest. She pushed me out of her way and went back to what she was doing while I reeled from her kiss."

"What's this got to do with the attic?" she asked.

"Patience, I'm getting there." I kissed her forehead, and she smiled. "You need to know the background before I take you up to the attic. With my words, I mean."

"Okay, Sir." She sighed. I liked her use of deference even if it was brandished like defiance.

"If you're going to be bratty I won't tell you any more."

"Sorry, Sir, I'll be good, promise." She sat up straighter.

I cupped my hand over her hip and squeezed. "So, like I said, Mum wasn't at all taken with the idea of me seeing a member of staff so when our interludes got longer, hotter and heavier we had to find somewhere to go where we wouldn't be disturbed. I literally searched the house top to bottom."

"What about the secret passageways?" India interrupted again.

"What did I say about interrupting?" I sighed tetchily.

"Sorry, Sir." She dipped her head. "But you knew about the passages, right? Why didn't you use those?"

I shook my head and loosened my tie.

"If you'd shut up I'd tell you. But no, you keep gabbling on. I think you're doing it on purpose, naughty girl."

"No," she insisted. "No, Sir, I'm not."

"Well, you won't do it anymore." I unlooped my tie and pressed it against her cheek. "I'm going to gag you so I can finish my story. If at any point you get uncomfortable with what's happening raise your hand and I'll untie you. Okay?"

"Yes, Sir." She nodded.

I gave her a couple of moments more, just in case she wanted to use her safe word, but when she stayed silent, I wrapped my royal blue tie around her mouth and knotted it at the back securely. I ran a finger down the back to check it wasn't too tight then cupped her face in my hands and dropped a kiss delicately in the middle of her forehead.

"Right, maybe now I can actually finish my story in peace." I kissed her cheek right above the line of the tie.

"So, as I was about to say, I didn't want to reveal the passageways to her because she might pass that information on, to Mum, to outsiders. I didn't want that at all. So I searched the house and believe me, that's no small feat. Finally, I found the attic, with the same warning sign that hangs on the stairs now.

"I cautiously ignored it, pushed on and discovered this. It was the perfect place to bring Ariana. It was here I discovered she had kinks. I mean, I was a naïve virgin..."

She snapped her head round to look at me.

"Yes, virgin. Anyway, I was just eager to fuck to be truthful and she was incredibly patient with me. I set up dozens of candles in here that first night. I thought it was romantic and you know, it looked spectacular. I didn't have a clue what I was doing, but she did. After we fucked—I'm not afraid to say it was a short and fairly straightforward experience—she asked me to pour hot candle wax over her breasts. I didn't know much, I thought it was weird, but if the lady who'd just happily taken my virginity wanted me to drip hot wax all over her then I was going to do it."

India made a noise, muffled by the tie, which I'm sure was an indication of arousal.

"She went crazy, bucking under the stream. I was fascinated how it went from liquid to solid on her skin. She had me pick the cooled wax from her skin as I fucked her—that was an interesting balancing act. I loved the red marks that lingered, my marks left on her, physical evidence of what we'd done. I realized then—the very first time I had sex—that it was better with a bit of kink. I also found out that Ariana was submissive. She taught me all I know.

"So I like to come up here and remember. Remember all the good times. Mum sacked her when she found out we were—well, I can't say dating, we never went on a date—fucking. I never saw her again." I looked away from India at that moment—I knew there'd be sympathy in her eyes. I looked back to check on her once I was convinced I wouldn't see it.

"So I keep some souvenirs of the old days up here." I reached over behind the pile of pillows and pulled out a coiled-up length of rope, a candle and a flogger and placed them on the blanket before India. "Would you like to play?"

India nodded.

"Good." I reached back again and after a little rummaging pulled out a box of matches and lit the chunky cream candle before me. "If at any point you're not happy with what's happening shake your head. I will stop the moment I see that sign. That will be your non-vocal safe word. If you understand and you're happy with that, nod now."

India nodded eagerly.

"Wonderful. Okay, stand up."

India stood, and I helped her kick off her shoes, then undid her top and pulled it away from her. I let her keep her skirt for the time being. I stroked over her shoulders and down her arms. I looked her in the eye and I saw a world of desire painted in her gaze.

"Come with me." I held her hand and walked her toward my favorite beam. It was the kind of beam developers hate. A little above waist height, it made walking through the middle of the room a pain. But I loved its old, weathered wood and the height was perfect for what I wanted to do.

I escorted India over to the beam and lay her arm flat along it.

"Keep it there," I said and walked round her to smooth the other arm flat. I stood back and flipped up her skirt. It was a beautiful sight—India bent forward, arse presented to me. "Don't move."

Hurrying across the floorboards, I picked up the rope and flogger in one hand and the candle in the other. I settled the candle just beyond her reach at the left hand side of the beam, then unwrapped the bundle of rope until I had enough to encompass her wrist. She twisted her head to watch as I tied then coiled the rope once, twice, three times around her wrist and the beam.

"Now, I could loop this over your neck and hold that down too but since you're gagged I won't do that." I just ran the rope underneath her and to the other arm.

She shifted and looked at me again as I wound the other wrist to the beam.

"Is that okay?" I asked, very much aware of how vulnerable she was and both turned on and grateful for her submission.

India nodded, narrowly avoiding hitting the beam with her chin.

"Good, if it gets too much just shake your head, don't stop shaking it. If I see that I will stop immediately, understand?"

She nodded, and I stroked down from the top of her head, through her long luscious hair onto her back and over her buttocks. The subdued moan she made intensified a moment later when I rubbed down between her buttocks and cupped her pussy in my hand.

"Wet already." I tutted. "I've barely touched you yet."

I wondered what to use first—the flogger or the wax? What a delicious decision I had to make. I took only a second or two to decide and picked up the flogger from the floor by her leg. I swished it in the air and her legs and back stiffened. Running the leather strands through my hand, I watched her, took in the whole picture. Her bound arms, the flickering candlelight, the focus of the torch holding her in the middle like a star on stage. The tips of the straps must have tickled her when I ran the length down her back because she wiggled. Well, it either tickled or she was begging for more. I decided the most fun interpretation was the latter and brought the flogger down with a flick of the wrist.

The crack echoed through the silent attic. I struck again before it had time to really dissipate. I had to build up the effort I put behind the whip of many leather tails to make it truly sting on impact. After three or four of my hardest strokes, India was moaning and bucking, trying to escape the crack of the flogger. When her cheeks pinked I stopped the punishment.

"Maybe in future you'll not interrupt and ask so many impertinent questions, India."

Pressing my fingers against her arse, I felt the heat there. Slipping them down between her buttocks, I found her hot, wet center. It amazed me how pain translated to pleasure for her.

"I'm not finished with you yet, though, India." She made a noise through the gag, maybe she cursed. I stopped fingering her. I knew she had to be vibrating with lust, I'd denied her an orgasm for so long. "I think you're going to like this next bit."

I traced a pattern up her spine and stepped over toward the candle. I swept her hair back over one shoulder and bared her back to me.

"I'll be watching carefully for your reaction, India," I whispered, reaching out for the candle and extinguishing it with a sharp breath. Slowly I tipped it. My cock bobbed in my trousers, reminding me how turned on I was. I let a few drops fall onto her back. She flinched, fought against her bonds for a moment, but she didn't shake her head.

I tilted the candle again, this time releasing a little more and watched the drip slip down and settle in a congealing pool at the base of her back.

"You will behave, India, you will. Remember you are mine to control."

I moved the candle until it was over her left shoulder blade. I poured the wax in a gentle, continuous stream like a cook drizzling oil into mayonnaise and left a diagonal streak across her back that ended at her waist above her right hip.

I did the same action but from right to left. A waxy X marked her back, marked her as mine. India seemed to be okay, no head shakes, but she trembled elsewhere. She'd done really well but I decided it was time to unbind her. I wasn't sure she'd ever experienced bondage before.

"I'm going to untie you now, sweetheart. You've taken your punishment well and now it's time for a treat."

Chapter Fifteen

India Grace

Tom had never bound me in our games of submission and control, he had just used his words to make me bend to his will. The rope turned me on and scared me all at the same time, and when Xander had stretched me along the beam and secured me I hadn't been sure if I was excited or petrified.

Then had come the flogging and the wax, and by the end of it I knew I liked it, I liked it a lot. It was a relief, though, when he unbound me, I had been nearing the edge of my limits. The rope left indentations in my skin, coils around both wrists that fizzed and popped as blood rushed back into my extremities, making me tingle all over. I could still feel the phantom tie in my mouth after he pulled it away and that imprint lingered, a reminder to be on my best behavior.

Xander captured my hand and dragged me back over to the blanket and cushions, pulling me down with him to lie side by side.

"Lie on your belly," he instructed, and I turned over to satisfy him. He picked off the dried wax, bit by bit, the sting reigniting.

"I can see a pink X right across your back, now," he purred and traced the outline with his fingers.

"I can feel it, Sir." I gasped.

"Good. Now, unfasten my trousers and suck my cock for me, my sweet, sexy slave. Show me how much you enjoy being mine."

Slave. I liked that, the way he'd said it, the way it resonated deep inside me. I'd always be his slave, even when I had to leave. We'd forever be bound together by these few acts of Dominance and submission and through years of history by that photo that had killed his father.

I couldn't dwell on that. I had a job to do, a very pleasant job. I focused on the now, unfastened his trousers and dragged them with his underwear down his legs as he lifted his bottom to help me out. I studied his cock, hard and straining, then dipped my head to plant a kiss on the very tip of him.

I loved the special brand of satisfaction that came from solely using all my talents to satisfy another. I had Xander in my control—his pleasure was dictated by my actions. I knew I couldn't tease him for long, though, I'd end up with another punishment. I moved around, climbed over his leg and settled on my knees between his spread thighs.

Bending forward reminded me of how I'd been bound—it stretched my back and I felt the pull of the wax burns, the X indicating Xander's possession of me. My body buzzed with arousal. I licked in a circle around my mouth and dipped my head downward.

I started at the base of his cock and kissed my way upward. The hard tautness contrasted with the softness of my lips and I couldn't wait to taste more of him, more of us. Not long ago he'd fucked me and I could detect my own fruity flavor along with his salty tang. I kissed around the fleshy rim of his dick and lapped up the juices that pooled there. I wanted more. I looked up along his body as I paused with my mouth just around the tip of him. He was propped up on his elbows, watching me.

I stared into his light blue eyes and sent him an unspoken message of desire before pushing down, stretching my lips around him. I covered the head and pressed the tip of my tongue into the dip there, rewarded by his gasp. I pulled up with a smile, took a breath and swallowed him again. I pulled him deeper before retreating. I kept on that path, taking a little more of him each time I delved forward until I could feel his pubic hair tickling the end of my nose.

I wanted more of him, more of his unique musk. I wanted to taste him, to drink down his cum, devour his pleasure. I felt his thighs vibrating beside me, heard his ragged breathing and knew he was close. I listened intently for direction but continued my ministrations. The pull in my back had become an ache but I ignored it, knowing his climax was so close.

"Fuck," Xander exclaimed and ran his fingers into my hair, holding me against him. He bucked up to meet me, his desperation forcing his buttocks up into the air, as he shivered and gasped. "Gonna come." His grip on my hair loosened but I didn't want to pull away, I wanted to drink him down.

I moaned around his cock and the vibrations trembled through his flesh. I was rewarded with a grunt then he stilled and I got the mouthful I wanted. Mellow but metallic, the salty liquid carried hints of chocolate and champagne. I eagerly drank, and Xander tightened his grip on my hair again and heightened my arousal.

He relaxed, unwound his fingers from my hair and stroked it instead. I let him for a moment, then, after one last lap of his cock, I raised up and straightened my back, moaning with the relief of pressure.

"Come here." Xander tapped the blanket beside him, and I climbed over his leg and lay next to him. He scooped his arm under my neck and pulled me close to him.

"Good girl." He leaned over and kissed the top of my head.

I smiled and just enjoyed being with him. We lay in companionable silence for a while. I rested my hand over his heart, comforted by its rhythmic beat, and he rested his cheek on the top of my head. I could have happily lain there forever.

"So, I told you about me and my discovery of kink. Tell me your story."

I didn't speak for a moment, wondering where to start.

"I mean, if you want to," he continued, "of course."

"I don't mind telling you," I replied. "I was just trying to work out where to start. I didn't know I was kinky until I was with someone who brought it out of me, but there were indications before that, I just hadn't noticed them."

"Like what?" Xander stroked his fingers up and down my arm, so gentle and tender, in complete contrast to the beautiful violence he'd earlier inflicted on my body.

"Well, when I first discovered masturbation I found it difficult to come by only touching my clit. It was only when I used my other hand to pull my hair or tweak my nipples that I managed to orgasm. From then on I would always incorporate a little pain into my play."

I snuggled closer to him, absorbing his heat, enjoying the contrast of his partly clothed body next to my nakedness.

"Ah, so who helped you work out you were kinky?"

"A man named Tom. He was a vet and I was his assistant for a while as part of work experience for university. He was significantly older than me but I had a crush on him the moment I saw him. He waited until the placement was over then propositioned me, or I propositioned him, I can never decide who takes the blame for that one." I chuckled against him. I'd never told anyone else about this, but I felt comfortable confiding in Xander.

"He was the first man to spank me. Classic, over the knee. I was surprised, too naïve to have discussed safe words first or anything like that. It hurt like buggery. I remember being close to tears but then beneath that there was this boiling arousal that just bubbled in the pit of my stomach and much, much lower.

"I was so wet, I remember him pausing the spanking to slip his fingers between my thighs and the low rumble of approval he gave when he felt how soaked I was. When he fucked me, my bottom stung and ached, a constant reminder of the spanking I'd received. It heightened the pleasure and I came so hard without even needing to touch my clit."

"Did you go out with him for long, this Tom guy?"

"Oh, we didn't go out. We fucked. I used to get the train up there at weekends. We never went on dates, we just went back to his and fucked."

"And was it always kinky?" Xander asked, tracing circles on my skin.

"Yes, always. I called him Sir, he spanked me with his hand or sometimes the back of a brush or a spatula, and he was in complete control. I did whatever he ordered. He never tied me up, though. Today, with you, was my first time being restrained."

"And…?" The question hung in the air.

"I loved it," I replied in a rush. "I loved being immobile and at your mercy."

"Good." He shifted, tipping toward me and pulling me into him. "I loved having you there, tied, gagged and wet for me."

Xander wrapped his left arm around me and stroked my hair. He tugged on it sharply, so I let my head fall back and he kissed the exclamation of pain from my lips. Just as his kiss deepened, my stomach decided to make the loudest, most disconcerting noise, which made him stop.

"God, sorry," I apologized.

"No, don't apologize." He lifted his arm up my back, turned his wrist and studied his watch. "It's almost four and we've not eaten."

"Already?" I gasped. My stomach rolled again, this time with disappointment. "I suppose I should get back on the road…"

"Or you could stay another night. It'll take you, what? A couple of hours' drive to get back to the city?"

I nodded.

"Well, by the time you get dressed and I feed you and whatnot it'll be late before you get home. You might as well stay here and leave first thing in the morning."

It didn't take much to convince me. "Okay, if you don't mind having me."

"Oh no, I could have you over and over again, Ms. Grace."

I blushed and giggled, and he kissed the laughter from my lips as my stomach decided to growl again. *Bloody thing, cock-blocking me.*

"God, we better feed you before you decide to eat me for nourishment."

"I thought I already had?" I quipped, and he chuckled.

"I suppose you have. Come on, let's find your clothes and get you fed."

It didn't take too long to gather my scattered clothing and put it on. Xander still held on to my underwear and while we walked back into the main body of the building I hunched up on myself, very aware of my swinging breasts.

"I'll go and get the food, you go and sit in the dining room," he said at the bottom of the main stairs.

"The posh one?" I asked, redundantly. It was the only one.

"Yep, might as well. We're less likely to be disturbed in there too."

Now that sounded promising.

The dining hall was a very big room to be waiting in on my own. The daylight was fading and the room was illuminated by the soft orange of the setting sun. I felt like a tiny, insignificant dot as I imagined the parties and the ceremonies that must have taken place there over the years.

The cool air brought up goosebumps on my arms. I wrapped myself in a hug and rubbed my hands up and down. I moved around the room in an effort to keep warm, past the tapestry that hid the secret passageway, along the length of the huge banqueting table. I wished Xander had let me go with him, I felt at a complete loss wandering around an impressive room filled with history that he owned.

Xander owned it all. It was easy to forget that when I was with him, but when I was on my own with my own thoughts it all came back to me in a flood. Who Xander was, whose son he was and why I really, really, *really* shouldn't be falling in love with him.

Shit, I'm falling in love with Xander.

Just as I thought that, in he walked.

"Now, it's not cordon bleu but it is food." He laughed. "And the surroundings should make up for any lack of excitement in the meal."

"Should I be worried that you are having to tell me it actually is edible? What have you brought?"

I walked down the length of the table toward him and finally I saw that he'd put down two plates with sandwiches on them. Next to the sandwiches was a packet of crisps and an apple. In the center of the table was a bottle of wine and two glasses.

"I kind of got distracted today, so didn't prepare anything for dinner. So this was the easiest and quickest meal I could come up with."

"It'll do me fine," I insisted. "Many of my meals at home look exactly like this."

Xander pulled out a chair and indicated that I should sit in it. He made sure I was settled then pulled the chair at the end of the wide table until it was closer to the corner near me.

"Dig in," he said. "Don't wait for me."

He proceeded to uncork the bottle, and I took a nibble from the corner of a sandwich. Ham salad.

"I brought a bottle of white, I hope that's okay?" he asked.

"Sure," I responded. "I'll have it whichever way it comes."

He passed me the glass, wide bowled and long stemmed, and picked up his own. He held it in salute, and I pressed my glass to his with a chink.

"To us"—Xander smiled—"and the things that bind us."

An image of being bound to the attic beam flashed into my mind and my glass shook from a salute to my lips. If only those were the only bindings in the relationship.

If I wasn't tied down with guilt how far could this relationship go?

Chapter Sixteen

Xander Patrick

India didn't answer my toast and my stomach twisted into knots with each sip I took from my glass. I'd thought we'd really connected throughout the day but mostly in the attic. It dawned on me then that maybe it was only me who'd felt that. Maybe to India it was simply a bit of fun and not the start of a relationship.

To even think of it that way made my heart flutter but that was what I wanted, what I hoped for. No one had ever made me feel like India made me feel. No one. I stared out of the window. The sun was almost faded, so I got up to grab a candelabra, lit the candles in it and placed it on the table to illuminate us.

"You make a good sandwich." India's words broke into my ponderings.

"Well, thank you. I have been practicing the art since I was a little boy." I smiled but I didn't think the action reflected in my eyes.

"I think you've perfected it," she replied, then took a bite.

I wasn't really feeling hungry, but I ate anyway. And I knew that wine on an empty stomach really wasn't a clever idea.

"It seems really strange to be eating butties in a huge room like this." She looked around in awe.

"It is a tad opulent considering," I replied with a smirk, "but this will be a sandwich you'll always remember."

God, Xander, maybe you'd like to confess your love next. Jesus, man, snap out of it.

"I think it will be." Her smile seemed a little off, like it didn't connect to her eyes, either. "Thanks for letting me stay another night, by the way, I'm not sure I said that before."

"Oh, you're welcome, India. Any time, you've got an open invitation to Mallard's."

At the rate I was going, I'd have proposed to her by the time she'd finished her crisps.

"I appreciate it" – she smiled – "but I rarely get to go back to the same homes, you know. *Good Manors* keeps me very busy."

And there it was – the rejection.

"Oh, I know," I bumbled. "I appreciate that but the offer is there all the same. We've all thoroughly enjoyed your visit."

"Thanks." Her smile did reach her eyes and there also seemed to be a film of tears there before she fluttered her lashes to stop them falling. "I've very much enjoyed my time here and really wish I could come back."

I reached out over the table and covered her hand with mine, squeezing gently.

"Well, the offer's open, any time at all. We'll always have room for you here."

India lifted my hand from the table and pressed it to her lips. I uncurled my fingers as she let me go and cupped her cheek. She cocked her head to the side and closed her eyes. Leaning over, I kissed her forehead.

"Would you like another drink?" I sat back, disconnecting before I said something stupid.

"Sure, that'd be great." She smiled and this time there was warmth in her eyes.

I relaxed. I might not have a long relationship to look forward to but we had the rest of the night and there was no use moping. I would use every moment we had left to revel in the joys of India Grace. I filled up her glass then stood the bottle back in place.

"And then shall we fuck on the table?" I asked with a wink as she tipped her glass to her lips.

She spluttered mid-sip and put the glass down. "Won't we damage it?" she asked, her eyebrows crinkled in concern.

"No, I think it can take a little more yet." I pointedly looked down at my crotch, and she barked a sharp laugh and shook her head.

"I meant the table." She chuckled.

"It has stood the test of two hundred odd years, I think it'll survive."

"Well, if you're sure. I don't want suing if a table leg falls off."

"I will take all responsibility for the wellbeing of my furniture," I said then nodded solemnly. "Though if you do break it that'll give me one hell of a good reason to spank your naughty arse."

"I'm not sure I want to imagine the spanking for breaking an antique like this." India shook her head. "I'd be a puddle on the floor."

"Well, let's see what happens." I was close to hard just thinking about fucking and spanking her. I pushed the plates away down the table, took a sip from my drink then shifted both our glasses away too. "Hop up."

The look she gave me was pure disbelief.

"Come on, India, don't make me ask you again," I barked, and she stood up.

I took her hand, pulled her toward me around the corner of the table then kissed her. I didn't think I could ever tire of the taste of her lips, the pressure of them on mine.

Pulling back from her, I tapped on the table with my free hand. She nodded, stepped back and slipped her bottom onto the edge of the table.

"Hold on. Before you get up there, take off your skirt."

Her eyes widened for a second but then she complied, revealing her lower body without a moment's more hesitation. India rested her bottom on the end again then wiggled back until she was seated and her feet dangled in the air.

"Now there's a meal I want to eat." I pressed forward, forcing her thighs to open until I bumped up to the wooden lip. Bending to kiss her again, I swept my hands into her long hair and pulled her deep into my embrace. She gasped against my mouth as our crotches met. I was hard, I was sure she could feel that.

I pulled on her bottom lip for a moment before kissing her chin and along her jaw line. Her breaths were already more like pants and when my kisses dropped lower onto her neck a rumbling moan reverberated through her whole body and into my lips.

I responded with gentle pressure then a bite. The moan turned into a grunt and she pressed her pelvis against me. I nibbled and sucked on the same spot for a moment and when I pulled away a little purple mark was left. I wondered if it would last. I continued kissing through my satisfied smirk.

Her skin was so soft and warm. I loved the contrast when I kissed over her hard collarbone and down to her soft chest. I stood tall for a moment and helped her out of her top. Her cheeks were flushed red and her hair was mussed up—she looked so delicious I dove right back in to kissing down her body.

I wanted to preserve the memory of every last dip and bump as I traveled her with my mouth. I might not get another opportunity to taste or feel her ever again and I had to relish every last second that I had. I wanted to be able to recall every moment of this erotic journey on future nights alone in my bed.

I cupped her breasts in my hands, admiring the bounce and the velvet softness with my fingers and mouth. She tasted so sweet, I couldn't get enough. I spent ages kissing around her areolae and nipples, feeling them crinkle and tighten to my touch. India keened and crooned when I finally drank as much of her breast into my mouth as I could. One, then the other and back again, I reveled in her soft plumpness.

Eventually the call of the rest of her body pulled me away. I lifted up and pressed against the center of her chest. Her heart was hammering. I didn't need to speak. She looked into my eyes and she knew what I wanted her to do. She lay back.

I looked at her for a while. Her brunette hair fanned out around her, the shocking pink tips no longer seeming wild to me. They were an indication of India. At first glance she hadn't stood out from the crowd but when I'd studied her further it had become clear that she had something very special indeed. Her cheeks were rosy red, she had her eyes closed in anticipation of what was to come. Her neck white, with one darkening bruise shockingly apparent just above her collarbone. I had marked her. My cock jumped at that realization.

My gaze swept lower, over her chest, the soft mounds of her breasts tipped with raspberry-red nipples that called to me to eat them. Bending over her, I took each nipple into my mouth one at a time, heeding their siren call. I dipped onto her stomach. She tensed, but I smoothed my hands over her hips and kissed across and down. Her stomach was beautiful just like the rest of her. Soft and giving with the cutest little belly button, which I couldn't resist dipping my tongue into. She giggled and wiggled her legs around me. I repeated the action and this time she moaned, tightening her thighs to my body.

I played with the indentation for a while, mimicking the movements of oral sex until she was writhing against me. Then I moved on, her legs stilled and she groaned in frustration. A wicked smile played on my lips as I continued my trail down her stomach and onto the soft hair of her pubic mound.

I kissed with gentle purpose, the curls tickling my lips and nose. Her thighs fell wider the farther I journeyed over her skin. I didn't know if it was a conscious move but it encouraged me lower, faster. Her warm fragrance made my senses reel with desire. She smelled of soft, warm bread and honey. I wanted to dive in and eat her up, to savor those flavors.

It was all about teasing her, showing her who was boss without restraint or punishment, and I wasn't going to rush. Darting my tongue down between her lips, I felt the bump of her clit then pulled back. She wriggled and gasped then lifted her hips to encourage me to do the same thing again. I didn't.

I ran my hands up the backs of her thighs and gently encouraged her to settle her legs over my shoulders.

She was wide open to me and I peppered kisses along one of her lips, careful not to graze her clit but to keep to the plump, juicy lip until it tapered out, then I kissed up the opposite one.

I continued this game until she arched her back and groaned with frustration. It was a test of my patience too. I wanted to properly eat her, bury my face and get lost in the scent and the taste of her, but it wasn't about my satisfaction, it was about driving her wild with lust.

I blew across her wetness.

"Oh, please," she groaned.

"Please what?" I asked, then blew again, directing the breeze across her clit.

"Please, Sir."

"What do you want?" I asked, lifting my head and looking along her body, taking in the tortured look on her face. She shook her head from side to side, battling with herself about voicing her desires.

"Tell me, India, what do you want?"

She opened her eyes and held my gaze for a few seconds. It was only when she closed them that she spoke.

"Please make me come, Sir."

"Good girl." I stroked her thigh as I praised her. "How shall I make you come?"

"Any way you like, Sir." She gasped and shuddered under my touch.

"That's a good answer, India, but how would you like me to make you come? What do you want me to use?"

"Oh God, Sir." She shook her head and scrunched up her eyes. "Your mouth, please, I want to come on your lips, your tongue. Please, Sir."

"That's better." I smiled and bent once again, giving her exactly what she wanted, exactly what *I* wanted. Her heat overwhelmed my senses, she burned my lips in the most erotic way, her intimate folds pulling against my mouth, rubbing, creating friction and yet more heat.

I made sure to lap at her clit, teasing the soft, silky protrusion with gentle licks. With each lash of my tongue it hardened further. India strained against me, her flesh pressing against my ears. I could still hear her moans and gasps, though, and felt her muscles tensing, her buttocks lifting off the table to push more of her into my mouth.

I pulled back from her clit and lapped at her slit. She tasted sublime—chocolate, fresh bread and apples. She was the tastiest, most satisfying meal. I wanted to eat her forever. India keened with frustration as I left her clit—well, I'd say high and dry but it wasn't, she was soaked—and I continued to focus lower down. I teased her lips, her sweet entrance, and reveled in her frustrated gasps and the fevered pumping of her hips.

Eventually I took pity, mostly because I wanted her orgasm, I craved it. Teasing her had been fun but I needed her pleasure. I returned my mouth to focus over her clit, sucking lightly and undulating my tongue over and around it. Her hips shot up and she ground her pussy against my face, pushing my nose into her flesh, surrounding me with her wet muskiness.

She was loud, so loud that I could hear her chants through the soft flesh of her clinging thighs. I kept the same rhythm with my tongue, letting her climb and shudder. I knew she was so very close and to deny her would be catastrophic.

She clamped around my head and she roared her completion, her wetness enveloping me. I clung on for dear life, lapping gently until she relaxed, her thighs dropping away, letting me up for air. I pulled away from the heat of her cunt and licked my lips. I was so hard I couldn't think of anything else but fucking her.

I fiddled with my fly, watching her all the time. Her eyes were still closed, her hands were thrown up beside her head and her chest was flushed red. She was replete and completely and utterly captivating.

As soon as I'd freed my cock I pulled her onto me, filled her in one long, slow sweep. Her eyes flew open and she moaned again. Erotic realization flickered in her eyes, the shock followed by the invitation, the need for more. She moaned, gasped and tightened around me as I sought my own pleasure, driven and motivated by hers.

I clung to her hips, driving into her time and time again. So turned on there was no hope of slowing down and pacing myself, I was desperate to come, and when my orgasm hit I couldn't hold it back.

I collapsed over her and she wrapped her arms around me, cuddling me to her chest. I was warm, worn out and content. Then I remembered she was leaving in the morning.

Chapter Seventeen

India Grace

Well, the table hadn't broken but I think I had. I held him close to my chest, we heaved in lungfuls of air in synchronization and I tried to piece myself together again. Every orgasm was destructive, clearing every thought from my mind, but the one I loosed on his lips lingered. I'd been close to coming from the moment my arms had given way in the bathroom. I'd experienced so much pleasure since then but hadn't come. I'd been buzzing with the need for it even before he'd spent so much time and energy on teasing me, bringing me to the brink over and over again. When I'd finally come I'd thought I'd never stop.

Why did he have to be so damn sexy? My job would have been so much easier if I hadn't liked him. But I was distraught at the thought of leaving and never seeing Xander again. I blinked back tears and wrapped my arms around him tighter.

"Told you it wouldn't break," he murmured into the side of my breast.

"You called it," I replied, trying hard not to show a trace of upset in my voice.

"I think we should probably move." Xander didn't stir. "Someone could technically walk in."

"How does someone technically walk?" I asked with a smirk.

"Technically," he extended the word. "I don't know but it could happen. We should move."

"Well, go on then," I challenged. "I can't go anywhere until you do."

"Okay." He sighed. "Just let me work out where my legs are and I'll get going."

I briefly wiggled my head, and finally he raised himself, pushing up on his arms that rested either side of me.

"Come on, one last room to show you tonight." He stood straight then grabbed my hand. He pulled me up and into his embrace. He gave me a quick kiss, stepped back and helped me until I was upright once more. I snatched up my top, skirt and shoes. He fastened his trousers, grabbed the candelabra and led me back into the secret passages, along to the staircase we'd used before and up to the first floor.

"I wish my flat had a secret passage," I mumbled, following him through the winding corridors. "Mind you, I've only got three rooms so maybe it'd be a bit redundant."

Xander laughed.

"Well, you can come and borrow mine any time you like."

"Thanks, that's quite possibly the weirdest offer I've ever had."

"I'm honored." He turned to me and winked. "Okay, we're here. This is one of my favorite entrances, come on."

He opened the door. Even after God knew how many years, the hinges were silent, and he waved me through. I nearly screamed when something brushed against my cheek but Xander was close behind with a light source and I saw that it was just a coat hanger.

"Wardrobe?" I asked.

"Wardrobe." He nodded. "Great, huh? But look at this."

He squeezed past me and pulled back a slat to reveal a filigree panel.

"What's it for?"

"Spying maybe, or checking who's in the room before letting yourself out? Looks like we've got the all-clear. Come on."

He pushed the door open and stepped out. I followed.

"I'm afraid it's candlelight only in here, it's totally like it once was—it never had electrics installed."

"That's okay." We were in the main master bedroom, a highlight of the guided tour, and I could see enough by the flickering light of the candles. "Are you sure we should be in here?"

"What do you mean? I own this place." He laughed. "Just stand still a minute, I need to take the light to the door and I don't want you knocking over an antique."

"That's just what I mean, what if we damage things?"

"We won't," he called over his shoulder, "don't worry."

I heard the grate of a key in a lock then the light came closer and Xander's face came into view again.

"The stuff in here is seriously old—"

"I know, India, I own it all. Don't worry." He walked over toward the bed, opened the cupboard beside it and extracted a small, cloth mat. He laid it on the cupboard and put the candelabra on top. "I've done this before."

I scowled. I didn't want to hear about his previous conquests at that moment in time. I was emotionally raw and I wanted the time with Xander to be just him and me, no memories or ghosts from the past.

"Not like that." He shook his head. "We've raffled off a night in this room several times to raise funds. We have lots of tricks to protect the integrity of the room while the winner is in here, lots of them we keep right here!"

"Oh, sorry for doubting you." I looked down at my toes sheepishly.

"It's okay. I was quite touched that you were so concerned for my antiquities."

Xander pulled me into his arms and kissed me then pushed me back onto the bed.

"Oh my God, the blankets…the original…"

Xander jumped onto the bed beside me.

"This is a very, very good replica of the real one." He grinned. "The original got too delicate to leave out about oh, eight years ago now. We got a replacement made."

I growled at him then laughed as he did.

"That was mean." I pouted.

"Yeah?" He stuck his tongue out at me.

"Yeah." I laughed and slapped his arm.

"I know, I know, but I do love seeing that scared look in your eye." He lifted my chin with his fingers. "It turns me on."

Before I could respond, his lips were on mine and I was drawn into a scorching hot kiss.

"It turns me on too. It turns me on anticipating, waiting for your next move, wondering what you're going to do to me, how it's going to hurt." I moaned.

He stroked my face, gently traced my lips. There wasn't time to hold back, there wasn't time to worry. I had to let him know what he meant to me because we only had one night and that one night was going to count.

"God, India," he groaned, "what are you trying to do to me?"

"I'm trying to make you fuck me." I grinned and pushed him back then I threw off my T-shirt and climbed on top of him. "Is it working?" I rocked against him, pressed my crotch down onto his, feeling the bulge there.

"Oh yeah, it's working." He gasped.

I laughed and ground against him some more.

He grasped my waist, and I continued to ripple my body, rubbing his crotch on each downstroke. Me with no knickers, him with trousers in the way. I didn't care, it felt so good, the scratch of his fly over my clit, the pressure of his cock rubbing between my pussy lips. I didn't know if I'd be able to get off but it sure as hell was fun trying.

"Ah, ah, ah," he tutted, raised his hands to my waist and flicked me to the side.

I fell onto the mattress then his weight was on top of me.

"I'm the one in charge, India, not you." He grabbed my hands and held them down above my head. He lifted his hands away, waited to see if I would move them, and when I didn't he kissed me.

He sat back on his heels and leisurely pulled my bra out of his pocket.

"It's not the rope I'd choose," he mumbled, "but under the circumstances it will do."

Taking my hand, he wound one end of the bra around it. He tied a knot and doubled it then leaned up and wrapped the other end around the chunky post of the bed and secured it.

I tugged at the bond and my pulse quickened. I wasn't going to be able to loosen it and I wondered what he was going to do to me.

"Now, for the other." He pulled his tie from another pocket and repeated the process until I was stretched between the two posts with him poised above me, looking down and unbuttoning his shirt.

"That's better," he mused. "Not that I didn't enjoy the feel of your cunt against my cock, darling, but we can't have you getting ideas above your station now, can we?"

When he'd discarded his shirt he leaned over to kiss my cheek then whispered in my ear, "If at any point you're not happy with what's happening just say your safe word, this is all for your pleasure, you understand?"

"Yes, Sir."

"Good." He brushed his lips over my cheek again. "Good."

He pulled away from me and stood at the side of the bed, facing the wall behind the impressive bed as he stripped. It was all very surreal, I'd barely thought about the surroundings when he'd been near me, but now he wasn't I drank in the dark red damask, the mahogany posts and the opulence of my surroundings. I knew what it looked like beyond the radius of the light from the other day and I was thankful not to be seeing it. I'd be completely distracted by the history. It already seemed naughty enough being tied to a priceless bed—if I could have seen the priceless room I might have said my safe word in sheer panic. One doesn't simply just fuck in a room of serious historic importance. I was sure that had to be in the stately manor rule book somewhere.

Xander was a beautiful man in or out of his clothes. I traced his outline with my gaze—the hard lines of his chest, the soft rounds of his buttocks and everything in between. I wanted to feel him, that body against mine. I wanted to hold him close but I was immobilized, I couldn't.

"So, what am I going to do to you now?" Xander pondered as he turned to face the bed. "Hmm, so many possibilities."

He slid onto the bed beside me and just looked at me. I craved his touch, the caress of his gaze made my skin tingle.

"You're gorgeous, you know." He skimmed his fingers over my chest and breast. "I could play with you all day, every day." Xander tugged the skirt off my hips, trailed it down my legs and threw it over the end of the bed.

He headed back to where he'd left off, stroking my stomach then lower to my thighs. I was just relaxing into it, anticipating the next caress, shutting my eyes to enjoy it more, when it stopped.

I flickered open my eyes and he was smiling wickedly at me. I bit my bottom lip and pondered what he was going to do next. He grabbed my ankle and tickled my feet.

"No!" I shrieked.

He laughed and continued as I flexed and kicked my legs to dislodge him from me. I laughed and growled in frustration.

He relented, but only for a moment, then he moved the tickling to behind my knee.

"No, please, no."

He watched me thrashing with an annoyingly smug smile.

He bent my leg back and continued to tickle my knee. I found it harder to kick and I was distracted by the fact that my buttocks were exposed. He moved to his knees and grabbed my other leg. The tickling stopped, one relief, but the tension built. I was completely exposed to him. Every inch of my most intimate area was open to him and he was gazing down at me ravenously.

Yes, he'd been in such close quarters in the dining room but somehow having my arms immobilized made me feel all the more vulnerable, all the more embarrassed.

"So." He shifted his grip so that he held back my legs with one arm, leaving the other one free to do, well, whatever he wanted to do. "India, since we entered this room you've doubted my judgment and you've tricked and teased me." Xander tutted. "Oh, India, India, India."

He shook his head and my whole body tightened. I gulped, my cheeks flaring with heat. My heart raced and I held very still. I jumped when he pressed his fingers to my butt cheek but he just gently stroked me, moving from one buttock to the other, even skimming over my dampening pussy.

He had to have felt me relax because he raised that hand and slapped it on my left cheek, and within a moment he'd slapped the other. I wriggled against him as he rained the blows down, careful to catch the full plumpness of my cheeks. The sting sharpened and I yelped and cried out with pain. Just when I wondered if I could take any more he stopped and stroked my flesh again.

"I love how your flesh pinkens, India, it's so fucking sexy."

I was about to thank him when he smacked my exposed thigh. I jumped—I hadn't expected him to hit my thighs—but he concentrated the next blows there until the backs of my legs stung and ached to the same level as my arse. I struggled to get away from him but he easily held me back, held me exposed and open for him.

After another short pause while I dragged in air and composed myself, he varied the locations of his slaps from buttocks to thighs and back again. Some spanks were hard and made me gasp, moan or curse, and others were softer. I wasn't sure what he was going to do next and I was wet and driven wild with wanting.

"Have you learned your lesson?" he asked, pausing with his hand in the air.

"Yes, yes, yes, Sir," I panted.

"Are you sure?" His hand dropped and I flinched, but the strike never made contact. I cursed him inwardly for being so wicked.

"I'm sure. I'm sorry, Sir. I'll be good."

"Oh, there's no doubt about that." He lifted his eyebrow and grinned at me. "God, I can feel the heat from your cunt from here." He licked his lips and shuffled forward. "How must it feel here?"

He pressed his cock in the crease of my arse and pushed it up. His balls dragged along my stinging flesh and made me buck. I waited for penetration, but it never came.

"Mm, this feels good." He moved back then pressed forward again. His cock ran up and down the groove of my buttocks without giving me any satisfaction. I whimpered. It so wasn't fair. I wanted him to fuck me.

He moved his angle slightly and the path of his powerful thrusts moved higher, spread my lips and very nearly reached my clit. I moaned and thrashed beneath him, the stretch of my leg and stomach muscles adding to the sting of my buttocks at each impact, and

I felt as if my whole body was connected with pleasure. I shook and groaned with every wave of ecstasy. Small orgasmic vibrations spread out through me and I clenched my internal muscles as the ripples bathed me.

"I think I might come here, all over your sweet cunt," he growled. "Shall I do that?"

"Please, Sir." I grew brave and continued, "Please, Sir, come inside me, fuck me, please."

"Hmmm." The sound had a casual air but the fevered thrusting of his hips betrayed that.

"I don't know, you were naughty."

"Please, Sir, I'll be good," I begged, straining against my bonds. I wanted to pull him into me, to grasp him and hold him and make him fuck me but with arms immobilized and legs bent so far back as to be virtually useless I was at his mercy.

"Will you be, though? Are you sure?" He thrust higher, the spongy tip of his cock hitting my clit.

"Yes." I gasped as lust exploded through my whole body at the impact and he continued thrusting between my wet lips and touching my clit. "Yes, yes, yes," I chanted. "I'll be good, Sir."

And when I thought I could be happy with this impact, when I could feel my orgasm mounting, he thrust into me, fast and hard, and I screamed out my paradoxical joy, fulfillment and disappointment.

"Since you asked so nicely," he panted. He still held my thighs back as he fucked me and I could feel him so fully within me because of the position and the stretch of my muscles.

"Thank you," I moaned. "Thank you."

I clenched my fists and held on. I wished I could touch myself, make myself come all over his cock. He pressed harder and faster into me—he must have been eager for his own orgasm. I just had to lie back and take it—I was under his control and I loved it.

Xander was repeatedly hitting spots within me that sparked off clenches and sighs. I moaned my pleasure right up until the moment he shook and ground into me with a loud exclamation of satisfaction.

"Thank you." He smiled, once he got his breathing under control. "Thank you, India."

He let go of my thighs, so I settled my legs around his waist and he pressed on for a kiss. It might have been a trick of the light but I thought his eyes sparkled more than usual, like he was holding back tears. I threw my all into the kiss he gave me, comforting him, thanking him, loving him. All non-verbally. It was the only way I could do it.

"I'll untie you."

I felt bereft when he moved away from me to the corners where I was bound. He released me from the posts, but left the tie and bra tied around my wrists. He drew them together in his hands and settled them over my stomach. He lay next to me, his head on my shoulder, one hand holding my ties, the other laying casually on my hip.

"I love having you tied up." He slipped his fingers over my thigh and down into the v between. I eagerly spread for him, I needed to come. "Greedy," he purred into my ear. "Do you need to come, my love?"

"Yes," I pleaded as he touched my labia.

Xander pressed down, his fingertips zapping my clit with the lightest touch, and I arched up off the bed. "Yes, Sir."

"Good girl." He rubbed again and set up a rhythm that knocked me against the mattress, his fingers on my clit, rocking up and down.

"Ask me, sweet slave, ask me when you want to come."

"I want to come," I blurted. I was so close, I didn't care that I did it so quickly.

"Are you sure?"

"Yes!" I grunted through gritted teeth. "Please may I come, Sir?"

He didn't respond for a few moments, and I felt the orgasm bubbling up. If he didn't stop fingering me, I'd come anyway and just when I opened my mouth to beg one more time he said three worlds that triggered an internal explosion.

"Come for me."

I shook and shuddered and with a few more strokes I came hard, the orgasm stretching out through me from top to toe. I curled up when the pleasure shrank back, then as he stroked my clit another time I threw my body out into a taut star of pleasure because another wave of ecstasy enveloped me.

I turned to face him—I needed a kiss, to be embraced, and he gave me what I needed. After a few moments of contented rest, he settled to undoing the knots at my wrists. He then kissed the light pink marks all over. I smiled and watched him pepper me with devotion, and slowly my eyelids closed. It had been a very tiring day.

Chapter Eighteen

Xander Patrick

I'd never had sex in the main show bedroom before and I was glad I'd done it with India. I had worried a little when tying her to the bed frame but both came out with nary a scratch. India had driven me to it, she was so wicked and wanton and I could be completely me with her. I'd had the most explosive orgasm and straight after I'd realized I couldn't keep her tied to me forever. I had to let her go. I could have cried.

However, I held back, untied her and made her comfortable. She was clearly sleepy so I pulled a blanket out of the bedside table and covered us both with it.

"We can't sleep here," she mumbled into my shoulder. "What if we're found?"

"Don't worry, we won't be." I kissed the middle of her forehead. "Just sleep."

"But if we're found together it could ruin the integrity of my story." She yawned.

"No one will find us together. Now sleep."

"Okay, Sir," she whispered, and I smiled. She was right, of course, it was all kinds of silly to fall asleep together especially in that room and on that bed but I didn't care. I wanted to spend our last night together actually together.

* * * *

When I woke, the sun was rising and suffusing the bedroom with a light glow. I looked at my watch—it was just creeping round to six in the morning.

"India"—I gently shook her arm—"it's time to get up."

"Mm?" she answered, stretched then finally opened an eye.

"It's time to get up and out of here, before we're caught."

"Oh yeah." She'd obviously processed all the information as she sat bolt upright, the blanket falling away and revealing her naked breasts.

My cock jumped.

"I better get clothes on and… Oh, can I have my bra back now? I need to get my handbag from your office too."

We got dressed and chatted at the same time.

"I'm going to go check on Harriet and the lamb, you coming?"

"Yeah, but we need to name Harriet's little one. You know, the poor girl needs a name."

India straightened the bed while I put away the blanket and cover. Then I noticed the candelabra had burned to empty during the night and I'd need to put new candles in it before putting it back in the dining room. I picked it up and carried it across the room with me to the door which I unlocked and opened. I looked left and right along the corridor.

"You're right, of course," I said to her once we were safely out of the room and heading toward the main staircase. "But it's not that easy."

"Okay, well, I'll help. How about Helen or Heather or Henrietta?"

"Why are they all H names?" I asked, measuring my step down the staircase.

"Because of Harriet, silly."

"I don't think I want a flock of H-named sheep, India. That's going to get complicated."

"Right, fine then. What about Lily or Nancy?"

"No, no, definitely not."

India sighed.

"I told you that it's not that easy," I replied with a chuckle. "You've got to get the name just right."

"Well, you suggest some then," she countered.

"Okay, I was thinking about maybe Madeline."

"The name's bigger than the lamb!" India exclaimed.

"Well, you're right there," I replied. "Or maybe Jane?"

"Oh, come on, poor lamb. Jane? What a boring name," she scoffed.

"I didn't hear you doing any better."

We bickered over names all the way to the barn via the office to pick up India's bag. We moved outside through dew-soaked grass and eager birdsong. Spring had definitely started spreading her charms as the soft heat from the sun had the first daffodils in bloom. I didn't want the playful banter to end, really, so I kept the name I'd already chosen a secret until we'd cleaned and spruced up the sheep's living quarters.

"I think I've got the perfect name," I finally said, leaning over the bars and watching the little one gambol around in the new straw.

"Oh yeah?" She was leaning next to me, smiling at the lamb's antics.

"Yep, it's special all right."

"Well, come on then, don't keep it to yourself, what's the name?" India looked at me, and I smiled back.

"Grace."

Her eyes lit up and she opened her mouth to speak, but nothing came out.

"You delivered her, so it seems only right."

"Xander," she squeaked, tears running down her cheeks, "that's so lovely."

I grabbed her into a hug and kissed her, her tears smearing onto my cheeks. I felt as if I could cry myself. When India left, Grace would be my constant reminder of her.

"Thank you," she whispered against my ear. "Thank you so much."

"You're welcome." I held her tightly. I didn't want to let go, I didn't want her to leave. "A little part of you will always be here at Mallard's."

She hugged me tighter, and I swore she sobbed into my shoulder, or maybe it was a laugh filled with tears.

"Yes, there will always be part of me here," she affirmed and kissed me again. "But you know, I'm going to have to leave now."

I nodded. "I'll walk you to your car. Then I suppose I better get on with running this place." I sighed, letting go of her when really I wanted to hold her tight, tell her I wanted her with me forever, but I couldn't.

"You do a fantastic job." She smiled and dashed away the tears from her cheeks.

We moved out of the barn, Harriet and Grace bleating their goodbyes behind us.

A few steps away from the barn, we ran into Graham.

"Oh, erm, morning, boss." He nodded in my direction.

"Morning, Graham, you're starting early today, aren't you?"

"Oh, aye, well, spring is here." He chuckled. The sound wasn't natural, it seemed forced. "Lots more to do now winter's buggered off."

I looked at him sternly, inclining my head toward India.

"Oh, pardon my French, miss. I thought you'd gone?"

"Bad traffic," she replied. "I ended up turning back and staying here another night."

"Oh, right, well, hopefully the roads will be clear today then."

Graham walked off before I could work out if that had been a nice gesture or an insult. He definitely didn't seem impressed at seeing India, or me, for that matter.

"I don't like that man, Xander," she said. "I just don't."

"Oh, he's all right. A bit abrupt maybe, but he does his job well."

India bent down and picked up a scrap of paper from the ground, scrunched it up in her hand then pushed it into her handbag

"Well, that's the main thing, I suppose." She shrugged.

We walked on in silence for a bit. The closer we got to the hall, the heavier my heart felt.

"Well," she said when we got close to her car, "I'll be in touch with the article when I've written it. It'll be by the end of the day, I have to have it in before deadline."

"Okay, cool."

"So if you can reply as soon as possible with any corrections—say I get the age of the building wrong or something—I'd really appreciate that."

"Yeah, no problems. I'll keep an eye out for it." I nodded and scuffed my shoe in the gravel.

"So, goodbye number two." I laughed.

"Yeah, hopefully this will be the last one," she replied then awkwardly smiled. "That didn't come out like I meant it to, it sounded mean."

"No, no, I get what you meant, it's okay." I went in to hug her, and she returned it. I looked round—no one was near, so I went in for the kiss.

She was startled at first but her lips warmed to mine, and before I lost all power of thought and self-control I pulled back.

"I know I shouldn't have done that but I couldn't resist." I grinned.

We both glanced around us and there was no one there, we hadn't been caught.

"I liked it." She smiled and ran a hand down my arm. "Well, Xander, I better go."

"Yeah, sure, it's been a pleasure."

"For me too." One last squeeze and she let go. She fished her keys out of her bag and got into the car. She fastened herself up, put the key in the ignition and turned it. With a little wave and a smile she was gone. Again.

* * * *

The rest of the day was a complete waste of time. I don't think I did any real work, just stared at my screen and remembered. Every two seconds I'd check for an email from her then get back to my memories, my memories of her. I knew it was impractical to think that

India and I could be together but I started to plan ways it could work.

It was difficult. Anything where I would have to spend significant time away from the hall just wasn't doable and I couldn't expect India just to turn up on my doorstep when I called. She wasn't a takeaway pizza. It became obvious that if I wanted India Grace in my life, my life was going to have to change.

It was about six when the email came through. Nothing personal was attached, just a brief email then the article. Which was stunning. She sang Mallard's praises and really brought all the people to life. I laughed when I recognized my friends and colleagues there. India definitely had a real talent.

I quickly emailed back.

All brilliant, even the picture of me isn't too horrendous. Thanks so much.

I spent a long time pondering how to sign it off.

What am I, a bloody teenage girl? Jesus, Xander, man up. In the end I put 'see you soon' and sent it into cyberspace.

Her response was disappointing.

Thanks, Xander, I'll let you know when the article is in.

Cold, abrupt and just about professional. It made me angry. We'd shared so much when she'd been here. I thought I'd met someone I could see in my future and she barely acknowledged my email. It didn't seem fair. I was convinced that she felt more deeply than that for me.

A knock on the door roused me from my musings.

"Come in."

In trotted Mary with a plate in one hand and a bowl in the other.

"I noticed you had nothing in for your tea, Xander, so I saved you some of ours."

"Thank you, Mary, that's very kind."

She put the plate on my desk, the bowl next to it.

"I've not seen much of you." It was a statement and a question.

"I know, I spent the day with India yesterday as I'd been such an absent host when she was meant to be here, and today I've been head deep in paperwork."

"We're keeping a track on things in the shop and there wasn't a penny missing last night or tonight."

"Well, that's good," I replied with a smile.

"Mm." Mary nodded. "I wonder why it's stopped now. We haven't done anything or fired anyone? Why stop?"

"Well, maybe they realized we were close to working out who it was. You've added in all the extra stocktaking systems. They probably think it's too risky to continue."

"Well, I hope so, sir, I really hope so. I'll keep you informed." She looked tired. All this suspicion and extra vigilance was wearing on her. She was naturally such a sweet and caring individual, it had to have been hard to keep thinking of everyone as a potential thief.

"Thank you, Mary, you're a star."

"Well, I do my best." She smiled. "Now eat up before it gets cold."

Mary stood over me until I put the first forkful of spaghetti into my mouth, then she nodded, wished me goodbye and left. It was only when I ate that I realized I'd not had any other food that day. I hadn't felt hungry at all.

I seethed quietly about India's email right up until visiting Harriet and Grace the next morning. I was so annoyed by her dismissal of me. How could she be so callous after all that we'd shared? I just didn't know.

But maybe I did. Maybe it wasn't just hard for me. Maybe she struggled with it too. It was a classic light-bulb moment. I couldn't bear to think that she'd not felt as much for me as I did for her. Maybe it was too much, maybe she'd been thinking things through just like me. Change was difficult. If she realized I'd have to break away from the hall to see her, break out of the twenty-four-seven routine of looking after the hall, my inheritance and how hard that would be for me then she'd know how much I'd have to give up for her. Maybe she didn't want to ask for fear of rejection.

I raced back to the hall and skidded into my office. On the computer was a list of all our newsletter recipients and I knew she was one of them. I scrolled through the addresses until I found hers, scrawled it down on a bit of paper then rushed out of the office again.

"Gerald, let Mary know I've gone out, will you? She's in charge."

"Yes, sir." Gerald nodded as I power-walked past.

I didn't have time to tell her myself. Mary would have a million and one comments and questions for me that she didn't really need to ask. She was a natural panicker. There wasn't enough time to reassure her, and she'd cope admirably without me anyway. Though truthfully, I just wanted to get to India – the hall could fall apart in my absence but in that moment I was uncaring.

Relief flooded me when the car started. I couldn't remember the last time I'd taken it out, but the tank was full and after a little cough and a splutter she ran beautifully. I kept my eye on the road but my mind was definitely distracted. What was I going to say to her when I got there?

I was an analyzer. I'd always done it. I'd take a situation and run though in my brain all the possible outcomes. I fixed problems by imagining lots of different ways of doing it and picking the one that seemed most likely to work. I spent the car journey imagining scenarios.

What if she wasn't in? What if she slammed the door in my face? What if there was another man in her flat? You name it, I thought it, and the farther away from the manor I got the more nervous I became.

Would it really be so bad just to have those few days with India? I'd always be able to remember them. Wouldn't that be better than an out-and-out rejection? But 'what if'… That was what kept me going. Hope. What if she felt the same way? Together I knew we could make it work. Between us we could come up with a plan.

My frustration grew, road signs were unhelpful and traffic grew heavier. I didn't do well in cities and remembered why as I crawled up roads at snail's pace and got turned around by one-way streets. Then when I found her apartment block there was the challenge of parking. Finally I got a space, turned off the car and sat still, staring through the windscreen.

What if…had powered me that far but it then started backfiring on me. I imagined all the negative reactions she could have and I wasn't sure I could face her. Could I face having my hopes crushed to dust?

In the end I decided. I had to know one way or the other, then I could move on. If I didn't go to see her then 'what if' would plague me for the rest of my life. Acutely aware of my heartbeat, I ascended the elevator to her floor. My mouth was dry, I kept swallowing and gasping. Terror enveloped me when I reached her door.

For one split second I contemplated running away but didn't. I knocked.

Chapter Nineteen

India Grace

Weeks of nothing loomed in front of me. I wouldn't be sent to a new manor for a while and apart from the Monday morning meeting at the office there was nothing for me to do. How was I going to survive at all with thoughts of him spinning in my head? I did my best. I'd only thought of him a million times since sending the email and done precisely no work. I kept attempting to but I'd get distracted by funny cats and stupid personality quizzes.

It was when I needed a pen—to write down the Countdown Conundrum—that I opened my bag and found the scrunched up paper I'd picked up at Mallard's. I unscrunched it.

Old Marsden's Place 9pm

Weird. Maybe it was a love letter from Jenny. That was her last name, so maybe she was arranging a rendezvous with Harry or something. I tossed it back into my bag.

I didn't want to think about Mallard's and certainly didn't want to think about Xander but I just couldn't settle to anything else. I slept fitfully, couldn't eat, didn't bother getting out of my nightie. It was only the knock on the door that made me even realize what I was wearing.

I ignored the first knock—it was either someone wanting to sell me something or a neighbor after a cup of sugar, but then the door rattled again with a more determined thump and it became clear that whoever it was wouldn't go away until I answered. I looked through the little spyhole in the center of the door and nearly fell over backward with shock.

"What the..." I struggled to open the door through my shakes, to find Xander staring straight at me.

"India..." He didn't say another word, simply walked forward and kissed me. The heat of the kiss was ferocious, making me gasp with the intensity. He pushed me back, knocking the door closed behind us.

"Xander," I panted. "Xander, what are you doing here?"

"Fucking you," he replied, looked around then thrust me backward again.

I kept kissing him as I retreated, caught up in the wonder of him being in my flat. In my untidiness, I hadn't been arsed to clear up.

"But you shouldn't be here, and God, I'm not dressed and we can't—"

He cut me off with another deep kiss and continued to maneuver me. The back of the sofa hit my calves. Xander kept on shoving, and I dropped onto it. He followed moments after.

"Xander—"

He kissed me again, a very effective way of making me shut up, and with the weight of his body squashing me against the sofa arm, I couldn't move, couldn't think, because there he was, on top of me, hot and hard and immovable.

"Xander—" I tried again. I had to try again. It was madness, wasn't it? Hell, it could even have been a hallucination for all I knew but I just couldn't let myself surrender. My heart was already breaking, how could this make it any better? We'd have to say our final goodbye a third time. I'd fall apart.

"Shut up, India." His lips pressed against mine insistently and it was impossible not to react, to press back.

His kisses were addictive. Xander ran his hands up under my nightie and squeezed my breasts. There was nothing stopping him because mortifyingly I was still in my nightwear, and God, I hadn't even had a shower. Xander didn't seem at all put off, even though my cheeks flushed with embarrassment. He was focused on one thing, the one thing he'd said he'd come for. To fuck me.

Lifting my nightie higher, he bent and sucked my nipples. I gave up fighting then—I was being flooded by physical pleasure and my mind couldn't cope with being negative anymore. Yes, as soon as the rush of endorphins ended we'd have to talk but until that moment I decided to give in to the madness, to give in to Xander's powerful lust and my longing for him.

My breathing quickened. He pushed a hand down over my stomach and lower. Xander kissed me again, long and slow, and when his fingers slipped inside me, he fucked me with the same rhythm and precision. All my thoughts centered on my clit. Nothing else mattered but pleasure—mine and his. The quest for orgasm replaced the search for knowledge.

I traced a one-digit pattern on his shoulder, and he dropped his kisses to my neck, all the time pumping his fingers between my thighs. I loved the push and pull, the sound of my wetness clinging to his digits and the shocks of pain that jolted through me when he changed from kissing to nibbling my flesh. I gasped and groaned at his ministrations, alive with arousal and desperate for more of him. I enjoyed his fingers in me, his lips on me, but I wanted more, I wanted all of him.

Just like he'd sensed my innermost wish he pulled his hand away from me then unzipped his jeans. I watched as he shoved them down his legs. Tracing the strong muscles of his softly haired thighs with my gaze, up to his hard-on, I moaned, eager to feel him within me.

It seemed he was equally eager because a moment later he was inside me. I hooked my leg around his waist and wrapped him close in an embrace. I didn't want him to leave, I wanted him to stay forever with me, within me, part of me.

We didn't speak, the only sounds were the creakings of my sofa and the labored rasp of our breathing. I couldn't look at him—if I did I knew I'd cry. I was so relieved he was with me. Part of me still wondered if he was a mirage, and the idea of letting go again, the inevitable parting, broke my heart.

I screwed my eyes closed and willed those thoughts away. I concentrated on the rhythmic pull and push of his hips, the scuff of his pelvis against mine, the throb of his cock within me. My pussy tightened around him, squeezed him harder. I dug my nails into his back as pleasure rippled through me. I clung onto him with everything I had, desperate to keep him with me, to show him what it meant to me that he was there.

"God, oh God," he groaned, his hips quickening, his thighs shaking.

He called my name when he came, arched and pressed into me. I held him closer, squeezed him to me. He relaxed and laid his head on my shoulder. The explosion of orgasm ended, the quiet sadness of inevitable heartbreak settled over me.

"Hello," I whispered, stroking his back.

"Hi," he replied, his words muffled against my chest.

"Why are you here, Xander?"

"Well," he replied between pressing butterfly kisses to my chest. "I thought that was rather obvious."

"Xander." The rough note to my voice showed I meant business. "Why are you here?"

"I missed you."

Tears bubbled into my eyes and I flickered my eyelashes to be rid of them.

"I missed you too but—"

"Don't say it, please, don't finish what you were saying. Not yet, please, not yet."

I stroked his back and we lay together in silence. Not a comfortable silence. We both knew we couldn't exist in the bubble that just contained 'I miss you'—we had to move on.

"But it can't work out, you and me." *There, I finished my sentence.*

"I don't think it's that black and white, India. I've been thinking—"

"You have the manor, Xander. It needs you. I have my work that takes me all over the country, in fact, there's talk of taking me into Europe."

"Do you not want me, then, India?" His question echoed with bitterness.

"Xander, it's not that simple." I sighed. "I want you, of course I want you, but there are things in the way, insurmountable things."

"I don't think they're insurmountable," he replied. "I can be a little less married to my job. Mary is perfectly capable of looking after things when I'm not around. She's in charge now. I can get away from Mallard's more often. It's just a case of scheduling."

"Xander—" I kissed the top of his head and gulped back all emotion.

"What, India? What? I don't understand. I want you in my life and I'm willing to change to make that happen. Why are you still resisting me?"

He pushed up and away from my body. Scrambled into his jeans. I sat up, pulled my nightgown right down over my knees and curled into the corner of the sofa.

"I have to, Xander," I finally whispered. "It's not just about scheduling."

He sat at the end of the sofa and worried his fingers together. "What is it about?" He ground the words out between his teeth.

I let the silence linger. I had to tell him the truth. It wasn't fair to keep hiding, to make more excuses. He'd see right through them anyway. Before I could speak he continued.

"God, India. I've had the best time with you. I've shown you so much of Mallard's, all the secret bits. I've shown you so much of me and all my secret bits. I've laid myself out for you, given you everything. Jesus, I'm here, aren't I? Is this all a waste of my time? Just tell me, India. Just tell me and I'll leave your life forever."

I looked up into his eyes and the anger that burned behind the brilliant blue hurt so badly that the tears I'd barely held back poured down my face. My body was wracked with sobs.

"Jesus, India, what is it?" He moved along the couch and wrapped his arms around me.

I held him close and cried. I couldn't form words, I couldn't think. It just hurt so much. It was all so very wrong.

He held me, ran his hands through my hair and let me cry. I fell apart—I'd been struggling to hold everything together. To hold back the guilt and pain, to pretend it didn't exist. I should never have let things go as far as they had. I should have shut it all down before anything had even started.

But I'd let him into my heart and now I had to tell him my secret. Let him know just what an evil, wicked woman I was. He'd never be able to forgive me. I had to tell him then I'd never, ever see him again.

"Tell me," he whispered against my ear once the sobs had quietened and my tears had dried. "It's okay, India, just tell me."

Pushing out of his embrace, I took a breath to steady myself. "Okay, I have a confession to make. Something I should have told you before... Well, something I should have told you."

Xander ran a hand through his dark hair then dropped it to his lap.

"Okay, tell me."

How did I tell him? I opened my mouth to start then closed it again. I lifted my hand to make a point as I started to talk but before the first word escaped my lips it faded and I ran my hand back through my hair.

"It's not easy." I looked at him. "I'm sorry, I know this is making it worse for you but I just don't know how to tell you this because it's going to hurt. Me, you, both of us."

"Take your time." He gulped. "I don't want to hear this but I know I have to."

"Yeah." The word juddered. I covered my eyes with my hand and slid it down over my cheek. "Okay. I'm just going to say it. I'm sorry. Before I say it I want you to know that I am so incredibly sorry."

A phone rang. It wasn't mine, and by the annoyed expression that passed across Xander's face, it was his. He reached into his pocket and pulled it out.

"I'll switch this off…" He glanced at the screen and changed his mind. "God, it's Mary, hang on."

"What is it?" he asked, not even starting with a greeting. "Shit. Okay, I'll be back as soon as I can. A couple of hours max. Call the police, tell them everything."

"What's happened?" I asked.

"Grace is missing." Xander stood. "I'm sorry but I have to go."

"Has she got out?" I asked.

"No, it looks like she's been stolen."

"Oh my God." I covered my mouth. "Who would—?"

Xander shrugged.

"I've got to go right now."

"Hold on, let me change, I'm coming with you."

"What?" He shook his head.

"You need all hands on deck and, God, I don't want to say it but you might need my veterinary skills. I'll be two minutes." I dashed into my bedroom. "Stay there."

I pulled on a pair of jeans and a jumper then raced back into the living room. Xander was just at the door.

"I'm coming." I grabbed my handbag and slipped on my ankle boots that stood near the door.

"Are you sure it's wise?"

"No, not really, but you need me."

Chapter Twenty

Xander Patrick

"I'm parked across the road." She jogged beside me as I speed marched to the car.

"What do you think has happened?" she asked once we'd maneuvered into the madness of the city traffic.

"I don't know, really. Who would steal a lamb and leave the mother?"

"Maybe Harriet was too much for the thief, I bet she gave 'em what for." India was doing her best to reassure me, I could hear it in her tone.

"She is very protective, she's given me a kicking for getting too friendly with Grace, so maybe you've got a point there."

"Any idea who's taken her?"

"No, not really. I mean, we've had some trouble with the shop lately, but I don't think it will have been one of the staff. It couldn't be, could it?" The idea seemed so wrong. The staff were virtually part of my family.

"I wouldn't think so. By and large I liked the staff, and those I wasn't so keen on still seemed devoted to the Hall. Has someone got it in for you, personally?"

"God, no. I'm too poor to have a nemesis!" I scoffed.

"It doesn't seem to make sense."

"Not really. I mean, Grace is worth a lot of money but there are so few Castlemilk Moorit in the country, keeping her for the wool wouldn't make sense, she'd be found eventually. Rare breeds have to be registered."

It was good to have India with me. But raw emotions from the earlier encounter lingered and I could feel an atmosphere around us I just didn't like. The situation with Grace was stressful enough without me feeling like I had to tiptoe around India too.

"We probably should just discuss this at some other time but I want you to know that whatever you confess, I'm sure it won't change my feelings for you."

"You have feelings for me?" she asked, an upward lift of doubt raising her tone.

"Of course I do, why else would I turn up on your doorstep like that? I've not been able to get you out of my head."

"Xander, can we just put the whole thing on hold for now? Pretend I didn't say anything at all." She sighed.

"If you can do that, I can do that." Or at least I could try.

"I'll tell you everything soon but I can't deal with that and help you save Grace. And I really want to save Grace. I love that gangly little bundle of fleece."

"Okay by me, India." I knew my reply was clipped but it hurt to hear her so easily confess her love for that lamb, the lamb I loved too, when I hadn't heard a word about love for me. I knew I loved India Grace, I just wished I knew it was reciprocated.

"Good."

We kept the topic of conversation light as we continued. The issue wasn't quite forgotten but it was pushed to the back of the queue, and though I was fully aware that we'd have to address it at some point, I was equally happy not to know.

* * * *

When we arrived at the hall, Mary, Jenny and Harry were waiting in the driveway for us and they all started talking at once.

I held up my hand.

"Let's get to the barn. On the way you can take turns to fill us in. Mary first."

"Well, nothing new to report, we still can't find her. We've had everyone looking for her but we are very sure she's not here at the manor anymore."

"Harry, anything to add?"

"Not really, boss. Just that I checked on the both of 'em around lunchtime and they were fine. I didn't see anything unusual. So it must have been after lunch that she got nicked."

"Thanks, Harry." I smiled at him. The poor guy looked really nervous, but then as one of the new guys he probably thought we'd all blame him or Jenny first.

"And, Jenny, anything you need to say?"

"Well, no, not really, I was wondering what India's doing here?"

Now that was something I'd not thought about when galloping back. Explaining that one.

"I managed to leave my camera here. Xander found it and very nicely brought it back to me. He was at mine when Mary rang and I wanted to come and help," India calmly lied through her teeth.

"Yeah." I nodded at her appreciatively. "And I thought the more the merrier, really."

Jenny seemed satisfied and we entered the barn. Poor Harriet was nuzzling around, clearly distressed to be without her lamb.

"It's all right, girl, we'll find her," I said. She responded to my voice with a bleat that was enough to break my heart.

"We've looked all over in here, Xander, we've not found a thing." Mary was using her placating voice. That irritated me. She'd already given up.

"But a new pair of eyes might pick up on something you missed. Let me look," I snapped back.

"Xander"—India scrabbled in her bag—"I've just remembered something, something I picked up when I was here. Well, just outside."

I walked over to stand beside her as she rifled further.

"Ah, here it is." She pulled out a scrunched up bit of paper and passed it to me.

"Old Marsden's place, nine p.m.," I read.

"I picked it up outside, not far from here," India added. "I put it in my bag, thought it was rubbish."

"Anyone know what this is?" I asked.

"No." Harry shook his head. "But that's Jenny's dad's farm. I don't think he's got anything to do with this. He's a nice enough bloke."

"It can't be me dad," Jenny squeaked. "And it's not me!"

"It's okay, Jenny," I reassured her. "I know it's not you." I didn't know that, of course, but I wanted to calm everything down.

"But it's worth checking this out. What time is it?" I asked.

"Six-thirty," Mary answered.

"Well, let's go. Will your dad let us have a poke round his place, Jen, just to check the thieves aren't hiding our Grace there?" I addressed her as part of our team. I didn't want her to think I was using an accusatory tone – we needed her to get onto Barry Marsden's farm.

"I'll ask him, I'm sure it'll be fine. We don't use a load of the old outbuildings so you'll be best to look there, first."

"Okay, Jenny, India, Harry, come with me. Mary, can you stay here and hold the fort?"

"Sure." She nodded. "Ring me the moment you find anything."

"I will." I smiled – having Mary to rely upon made my life so much easier.

"Okay, well, good luck." Mary smiled and nodded reluctantly then left to go back to the house. I walked out of the barn, the others following, and headed toward the car.

"Thanks, India," I said when I noticed her walking beside me.

"I've not really done anything." India shrugged.

"Well, you picked up the litter and if you hadn't we wouldn't have this tip-off."

"It might not be a tip-off." She laughed uneasily.

"But it might be, and it's something. I don't know what we'd have done otherwise."

"Well, I hope it's useful, I really do."

"Me too." I didn't know what else to add. An awkward silence fell over us and I was thankful when Jenny walked up and started to chat to India and I didn't have to think of anything else to say.

It was an interesting car journey – Jenny and India sat in the back chattering away and Harry sat beside me on the passenger seat. He was never a brilliant conversationalist so I wasn't surprised when he didn't say a word.

"I'll go talk to me dad, wait here. He can be a bit funny with strangers on his land."

Jenny leaped out of the car and ran over to the small farmhouse, yelling all the way. Marsden's farm was a familiar sight. I'd been there to pick up stock since being a child. The only change was the degradation, the growing weeds and the weathered plaster.

I wanted to move off and look around but I knew that would be a mistake. Upsetting Barry would make a huge dint in the profitability of Mallard's farm shop. Anxiety lay in the pit of my stomach, and not just about Grace. Once all the fluster of the kidnapping, lambnapping, whatever you'd call it, died down, I knew I'd have to face India and her confession, and I really didn't want to.

"Dad says we're all right to look round. Said he's not seen owt but he was up in the top field all today so he wouldn't have." Jenny bounded back over to us.

"Well, I think we're best to search the outer buildings and barns first. If they're hiding Grace here I'm certain that's where she'll be." I nodded. It was already seven o'clock—we only had a couple of hours left.

"Okay, me and Harry will go to the right, you and India work out to the left." Jenny grabbed Harry's hand and was hurrying off before I could say another word.

"Well, looks like it's me and you then." I smiled at India who returned it awkwardly. I'd have split us up if I'd been deciding the teams. I wondered briefly if it was weird for Jenny to split herself away with Harry. Maybe I should have insisted on her staying with me and India partnering Harry. A trusted person in each camp. I couldn't believe I was thinking that about those two but all this madness was making me even less trusting than usual.

"This place is huge." India gasped. "Look at all these buildings."

"Back in the day, Marsden's supplied beef and milk for the entire county and beyond. Business is still going but it's not robust. The prices of beef and milk have come down so much and the big suppliers aren't able to give as much back to the farmers. Barry's moved into artisanal seasonals to bulk up his income. His herd's dwindled considerably."

We headed into the first barn, which was in relatively good repair. It was obviously one of the buildings they still used.

"It's his business with us at Mallard's and other independent suppliers that keeps him in business."

"That must feel good." India moved into the barn and looked around the machinery, peering underneath and giving me a fabulous view of her arse encased in denim.

I inhaled sharply and shook my head. I didn't have time to be distracted by desire.

"Yeah, yeah it does." I nodded.

"No sign of her in here." India sighed.

"I guess that makes sense." I let her pass me and exit the barn ahead of me. "This is a working barn. If Grace is here, she'll be somewhere quieter."

We checked the next few outbuildings with no luck and not much in the way of conversation. As we got farther from the farmhouse, the buildings became more run-down, with chipped paint, broken windows and trees and weeds growing in, up and around them.

We had pushed and pulled our way through two of them and stood outside the last visible building, wiping sweat and muck from our brows.

"What was that?" India placed her hand on my arm.

I stood stock-still but my heart thumped madly at her touch. All I could hear was the rushing of my blood, no matter how hard I strained. I was about to break the silence when I heard it too. A little bleat.

"Barry doesn't keep sheep, that must be Grace."

We rushed to the last building, heaved the wooden bar blocking the double doors out of the way then I carefully pulled the rotting door open.

"Grace?"

The barn was dark, lit only by a few high skylights. There didn't seem to be an electricity source at all. I could barely see where I was walking.

"Hang on." India fished in her bag and pulled out her mobile. She swished her finger down the screen and activated a light. "I knew the torch feature would come in useful someday."

I walked next to her, keeping to the pool of light. We heard the bleating again and headed toward it. In the back corner, we found a cage, and inside that cage was a trembling Grace.

"Bastards," I growled. The lamb was in a bare cage, no water or food. I unlatched it and pulled Grace into my arms. She nuzzled up against me.

"We need to get her some water."

We headed back to the farmhouse and stopped by an old outside tap to give the thirsty lamb a drink. She lapped gleefully from my cupped hands.

"Who the hell would keep her in here?" Harry shook his head when we met them back at the farmhouse.

"I don't know." I sighed. "I can't believe it's someone who lives here."

Jenny shook her head vehemently. I didn't want to think it was her or one of her brothers but who else would be able to get on old Marsden's property without raising the alarm?

"Shouldn't we wait here and see who comes to get her?" India asked.

"I'm not sure that's wise. What would we do when they turned up? They might be dangerous."

"We should call the police." Harry nodded. "Mary rang them to report Grace stolen, we should tell 'em where we found her and about the note."

It was a good plan, and while the others looked on I rang up the local police station and updated them.

"Okay, they're going to send a few officers up to check it out."

"I'll let me dad know," Jenny chirped. "I'll be back in a minute."

I danced from foot to foot agitatedly until she got back. Grace needed to be back with her mother, she needed Harriet's milk. Jenny was as quick as her word and we were soon in the car and heading back home. India sat in the passenger seat this time, Grace cradled in her lap.

Back at Mallard's, I sent Harry and Jenny to tell Mary the good news and India followed me up to Harriet's barn.

"I should probably go home," she said. "I could get a taxi."

"No, no, stay," I insisted. "I'll drive you home in the morning."

"Xander—"

"Look, India, I don't care what it is you think you've done. Honestly, you could be a convicted murderer and I wouldn't care."

India's eyes widened and she looked like she might be sick.

"I like you and we're good together. Really good together. I want to explore that, get to know you more. Please stay."

India sighed. The conversation stopped as we walked into the barn and Grace and Harriet both went mad. As soon as I set the lamb down in the pen she ran over to her mother who fussed and bleated and sniffed and snuggled her.

"Aw," India sighed. "I'm glad they're back together."

"Yes, and hopefully they'll stay that way now." I sighed.

We stood side by side, watching the pair frolicking then Grace suckling from her relieved mother. We'd stood side by side watching them like this several times before, and remembering those happier times, I wanted to reach out and touch her, hold her close.

"So, will you stay?" I asked her again, not looking at her, staring straight ahead.

"I don't know, Xander, I don't think you'll like me once I tell you—"

"Then don't tell me. Just don't. I don't need to know. I've got all the information I need. You're gorgeous, funny, kind, you like me tying you up and spanking you, I don't need to know anything else. Please stay. We can talk about the future tomorrow but tonight I just want to be with you."

"I'll stay," she said, then quickly followed it up with, "because it's getting late, but I need to tell you—"

I silenced her with my lips. I didn't want to hear anything else—why ruin something good with something potentially awful? I'd kiss her every time she tried to mention it if I had to, forever if she'd let me.

I pulled her tighter to me, felt her arms wrap around me, and sensed extra heat in her kiss when her phone rang, blasting Dolly Parton's *Nine to Five* into the air.

"Crap, I have to get that! It's Maxine and she only rings in an emergency." India disentangled herself from me and lifted the mobile to her ear.

"Hiya, yeah, yeah, I remember that." She nodded and smiled at me. "Really? No way. That's awesome! Now? Like, now?" Her brow screwed up in agitation. "Well, I'm at Mallard's. Yeah, I did but I came back. I'll tell you about it when I see you. Okay, are you sure? All right, that's great. I'll only need five minutes to pack a case then I can be off. Okay, cheers, cheers, bye!" She hung up then turned back to me. "I'm going to have to go. Maxine has ordered me a taxi, I'm sorry, Xander."

"No, it's fine." I looked down at the floor and shrugged like a sulky little boy.

"We've got the opportunity to go to a royal residence – it's not something I can either talk about or not go to. We've been working to get this for years."

"Sure, no, I do understand." I smiled up at her. "I'll see you soon, though, yes?"

"As soon as I'm back I'll arrange to see you." She nodded. "Promise."

What more could I ask for, really? She couldn't help her job and I couldn't hold her back. The small talk was strained and painful but when the taxi arrived a little later we parted with a hug at the front of the manor. I couldn't wait to see her again.

At eleven o'clock that night I got a phone call from a police officer who had news about the sheep hustling and he was stood on my doorstep.

"Hello, sir," he greeted me, and I invited him in.

"Hi, so you caught someone then?"

"Yes, we did."

I escorted him to my office and there he told me briefly what they'd found. I could barely believe what I was hearing.

"So it was Graham Taughton who turned up?" I asked.

"Yes, and we found Gerald Wheatley sat in a van just down the lane."

The van had contained several carcasses and a box of conserves and oils that had clearly come from Mallard's farm shop. The police were still questioning the pair, but it seemed they had not only found the thieves who'd stolen my lamb, but the men who were behind the fall in profits at the farm shop.

I didn't understand why, though Graham was a grumpy bastard and Gerald had never liked me. I answered the officer's questions, and after an hour he left. I'd have to fill Mary in with the details in the morning. It didn't make sense, and I now had two positions to fill immediately. How we'd cope the next day with tours I didn't know.

Even though I had all that to sort out, India was on my mind constantly over the next few days, especially as the newest copy of *Good Manors* had hit the shelves, creating a surge in visitors I could barely believe.

The article was really positive, and Mary kept reading bits out at me whenever she could. She was like a proud mother hen, telling anyone she saw that she'd gotten a personal mention in India's article.

"We're good friends now, you know." She'd nod. "She'll be back soon. She loves it at Mallard's."

I could only hope it was me that brought her back, not just the house. Everything was going really well, I'd had several comments about how much I was smiling. I sorted out the staffing problems by discovering that Harry was not only capable of talking to people, he had a brilliant memory for historical facts. He was doing really well as the new tour guide. I was even thinking of employing more staff, it had become that busy.

It was one afternoon, a few days after the magazine had come out, when the phone went. I answered professionally because generally anything that made it through to me was important business.

"Hello, Xander Patrick speaking, how may I help you?"

"How could you do it?" a reedy, wheezy male voice asked accusingly. "How could you?"

"Wait, do what?"

"You don't know?" The incredulousness of the tone was easy to identify.

"No, I don't know what you mean, Uncle Carl. It is you, isn't it?"

"Yes," he confirmed.

Oh great. My dad's brother rarely rang and when he did it was to complain or to demand something. I didn't have much time for the man who'd stood by while my father had drunk himself to death then blamed my mother for it. He was a nasty old curmudgeon.

"I know you have no regard for your father's memory, Xander, but this is beyond the pale."

"What do you mean? I don't understand?" I was close to slamming down the phone on him, except I knew the nasty piece of work would just keep ringing back until he'd made whatever point he had stuck in his mind.

"God, you are thick, Xander. I heard about the buzz at Mallard's, how you'd got an article in that magazine. Well, I had to take a look, didn't I, but I couldn't believe it when I read the name of the journalist."

"India Grace?" I asked with a shake of my head, looking back down at the invoice before me, determined to do some work while he twittered on.

"Yes, that evil harlot."

"Steady on, Uncle. India was lovely."

"I can't believe you've forgotten, Alexander. I really can't. I know you were but a youngster when your dad passed but I thought you'd remember the name of the journalist who killed him."

"What?" I shook my head in disbelief.

"India Grace took the photo that lost him everything. She took that evil photograph. That's what killed him, Xander. His reputation was in tatters after that. It broke him. And you let that excuse for a woman into Mallard's."

"I didn't know," I replied. "I had no idea."

"Well, now you do. I'm ashamed of you, Alexander Mallard. I didn't think even you could sink so low."

The line buzzed, and I stared into space. I didn't care that my uncle was angry with me, that was pretty much par for the course. But he couldn't be right—India couldn't have taken that photo. It had to be a lie.

It took a bit of digging, but an Internet search on my dad's name and hers did eventually come up with the evidence that proved he was right. That photo, those glassy, empty eyes, stared back at me. That photo was hers. She'd sold it to the newspaper. I even emailed them for confirmation. They got back to me quickly with an affirmative. She'd taken it. She'd ruined my father's life, broken my mother's heart and denied me the chance to make my father proud. India had thoroughly broken my family apart.

Chapter Twenty-One

India Grace

Windsor Castle—Maxine had got me in at Windsor Castle. It was such a whirlwind of activity as they had a state visit expected so they wanted me in and out sharpish. They weren't really in need of the advertising—visitors love anything royal—but they had a new section of the place on display and had decided *Good Manors* was an effective way to get news out about that.

The news had come at a key moment. I'd vowed to myself I wouldn't do anything else with Xander until he'd heard my confession. I couldn't. So I either had to tell him or leave and that wasn't a decision I'd wanted to make. Having to race off had saved me from that. I was completely absorbed in my visit but even so I found him sneaking into my thoughts all the time. I'd never be able to look at a four-poster bed in the same way for a start, or any kind of large jug.

It was on my last day at Windsor that he rang. The first time I hadn't been able to answer as I'd been in the middle of some intricate topiary with the head gardener. I had checked the call when we'd finished and sent him a text saying I was busy and if he rang back in the evening I'd be able to answer him. I'd just climbed into the incredibly soft and luxurious bed I was staying in when my mobile rang.

"Hey," I answered with a smile when I saw his name across my screen. "Sorry I couldn't answer earlier. I was in the middle of a bush." I chuckled at my own joke. "How are you?"

"Why didn't you tell me?" Xander's voice was hard and pained.

My stomach sank. "What do you mean?" I asked, even though I was fairly sure I already knew.

"My Uncle Carl rang and told me. I looked it up to be sure. I couldn't believe you would do something so sleazy. But no, he wasn't lying. You took that photo of my dad, didn't you?"

I sighed and ran my fingers through my hair.

"I was going to tell you, Xander—"

"After we fucked. After we connected… After you used me."

"No." I sat bolt upright in bed and shook my head. "No, Xander, I didn't do that. I wanted to tell you, I really did, but I didn't know how to. I didn't even realize you were Lord Mallard at first."

"Whatever, India. I thought you were different." The bitterness in his tone twisted in my heart and tears dripped over my cheeks.

"I'm not like that now. I was stupid and young and easily influenced. Lydia, my editor, told me I needed to do it, that it would be good for my career, and I did it. I did it without thinking and I've regretted that every day of my life since."

"Yeah, whatever." The venom stung even through the phone line.

"Xander, really, I didn't want—"

"I don't care anymore, India. I thought— Well, it doesn't matter what I thought, does it? You've trampled all over my trust. Don't contact me. I don't want to hear another word from you."

"No, Xander, please!" I begged. Sobs wracked me, tears cascaded down my cheeks. But the phone went dead. I dropped the mobile out of my hands and buried my face in them instead. Curling into the feather eiderdown, I cried. Hot, bitter tears of regret.

I didn't sleep properly all night. Every time my tired, achy body slipped into dreamland I saw Xander's father, his dead eyes staring at me accusingly. I'd totally screwed up. I should have said something earlier. A voice deep inside ranted accusingly at me. I should have stayed away, I shouldn't have got involved, and I certainly shouldn't have fallen in love.

* * * *

It was a good job that I'd practically finished everything I needed to before going to bed the night before because I was close to useless in the morning. I took a few photos, every one as lackluster as the last. I pasted on a smile when I said goodbye to the staff who'd become friends over the past few days but the moment I pulled away in the taxi my face fell and I was fighting to hold back the tears again.

Back at my flat, I spent a lot of time staring at my phone, at his number, wondering whether to call. Each time I convinced myself I should—what we'd had was special and I didn't want to lose that—I'd hover my finger over the Call icon but before I could press it I'd change my mind again. I repeated the same process over and over and over but never called.

I shouldn't have even engaged with him in the first place. It was surely better for both of us if I left him alone to get on with his life. How could he ever look at me again knowing what I'd done?

I couldn't concentrate on anything, though. I tried to write up my ideas for the Windsor article, something I liked to do as soon as possible, and I found it tough going. I wrote, though God knew what drivel it was. Each sentence was like poking myself in the eye with a hot needle. I couldn't even distract myself with my work, something I would normally find easy to get absorbed in. Every word I typed morphed into 'sorry' on the screen.

I was sorry—a sorry mess of an individual. With no one to talk to, no one to commiserate with me. It wasn't often I felt I needed anyone. I was quite happy keeping myself to myself for everyone's own good really. I should have kept to that way of life, should have ignored the sparks of attraction.

Yes, I'd had the best days of my life with Xander. I'd finally felt complete and even happy but I'd known it would end badly so why had I let it continue?

A second night of fitful sleep made it even harder to concentrate on the Windsor article. I knew I had to get it finished and sent in, though. Maxine would expect it and the last thing I needed was to piss off my boss too. I drank too much coffee and ordered in greasy pizza. The delivery guy looked aghast when I answered the door. Clearly I looked as bad as I felt.

I sat at my desk and tip-tapped at the keyboard, writing and deleting, deleting and writing until I finally had something I was vaguely happy to submit. It wasn't my best piece, but it was positive and I had some lovely photos to go with it. That was all I cared about.

After I sent it, I crawled back into bed. I didn't know what time it was, couldn't be arsed checking, but the sun was fading and I knew I needed sleep. I knew I didn't want to face anything anymore. I couldn't. My heart hurt so much that it was numbed to it. I was a shell. Incomplete and crumbling.

* * * *

Xander was yelling at me, his face contorted with anger, his hands fisted by his side. I was scared and crying and I ran. I ran away from Xander and his anger. I was moving so slowly, like the air was grasping my legs and preventing my movement. When I glanced back, Xander was a matter of steps behind but he wasn't on his own, his father was with him. I screamed and tried to speed up but I couldn't. I was getting slower, it was getting harder to move.

Filled with anticipatory dread, I glanced over my shoulder, and when I saw what pursued me, I screamed long and loud as the crumbling, rotting zombie corpses of Xander and Lord Mallard reached out and grabbed at me.

When I woke I was drenched in sweat and the bedclothes were twisted and wrapped around me like I'd been wrestling with them. I dragged myself up and into the shower. I closed my eyes as the water beat down on me. Remembered the old-fashioned bath and the promise Xander had made to me to let me bathe in it. I cried, or I tried, but it seemed I had completely dried up. Harsh, dry sobs shook my body and my throat rasped painfully.

Every action seemed to remind me of him and in the end I couldn't take it anymore. I picked up my car keys, threw on a jacket and left the house. I had to at least attempt to explain properly. To tell him how very sorry I was and to at least try to put things right. It would serve me right if he didn't forgive me but if I didn't try I'd never know.

It was a miracle I didn't get pulled over on my drive to Mallard's. It wasn't my best idea. I was anxious and speeding and also still very tired. But somehow I got to the Hall in one piece. I think my guardian angel flopped in a pool of sweat when I scuffed up the gravel on the drive and parked with a screech.

I wasn't sure where Xander would be, so I headed to the shop where Mary was busy serving a queue of people.

"Oh, India!" she squeaked happily. "It's good to see you!"

"You too, Mary. Where's Xander?" I probably should have stopped for small talk but I didn't have any desire to do so.

"Oh, I'm not sure, love. He's been in a right old mood lately. He'll either be in the office or down with Harriet, I reckon."

"Okay, thanks, Mary."

"Don't go without talking to me properly, okay?" she called as I turned and walked away.

"Okay," I replied, promptly forgetting the promise. All I was focused on was finding Xander.

I started at the office—he wasn't there. I went to Harriet and Grace's but he wasn't there either. I bumped into Jenny on my way back to the Hall. She greeted me with a hug.

"Do you know where Xander is?" I asked.

"No, I've not seen 'im today. He's been a right grump lately. I dunno what's up with him."

"Okay, well, thanks." I smiled and walked on. I went to check his bedroom, but he wasn't there. So I acted on an impulse and headed for the library. I was certain I'd found him before I entered the room as I heard noises of renovation. Bangs and cracks and scrapes.

I walked in to see him in blue overalls bending over a set of shelves, a hammer in his hand.

"Hey," I greeted. Probably should have made sure he'd put the dangerous weapon down first, but I wasn't thinking.

"What are you doing here?" He scowled at me then looked back to the shelves in front of him. He was attaching a new shelf, to bring it back to useable condition.

"I've come to speak to you." I sighed, shut the door behind me and purposefully strode forward.

"Well, you can go away again. I'm not interested in listening to it, any of it," he snapped and hit the newly affixed shelf with his hammer. It shook, but didn't move, give or break.

"Xander, I know you're angry and I understand why. All I want to do is explain. I'll go away then and you'll never see me again. I just need to explain."

"Jesus, India, why do you have to make this so much harder than it already is?" He shook his head and turned his back to me to look through a beaten red metal toolbox.

I didn't answer, how could I? I almost left but my sheer bloody-mindedness took over.

"I was twenty-two and really new to the business. I worked freelance for an agent who was cruel and ruthless. I should have told her to stuff it but I didn't know I could. I thought I needed her, that no one else would employ me. So I stuck with her. She told me the only real money in journalism was for sleaze. She gave me an address, what she expected I would find there and told me to go.

"I did fight back a bit, but the woman convinced me it was for the best. What harm could I really do? And I didn't know any better. I felt bad taking the photos. It felt wrong, invasive."

"Why didn't you stop then?" Xander growled.

"I've asked myself that question so many times. I'm still not totally sure but I think the fear of failing kept me going. If I didn't make it as a journalist then my family would be so disappointed. My mum wanted me to be a vet and I gave up on that. I thought I had to be a journalistic success and Lydia had convinced me that taking those photos was the only way I'd get that."

"When I found out he'd died so little time after I'd snapped what I snapped I was mortified, more than that. I was distraught, inconsolable. I told Lydia where to stick it and just retired away from the world. I know you don't care, that my pain was a fraction of what you must have felt—"

"I lost my *father*, India. He wasn't the best, but he was the only one I had. And it broke my mother. It left us virtually penniless and in control of this place. You bet you don't know the pain I felt." He turned and scowled at me.

"I was sorry, though, Xander, so sorry it nearly broke me. In fact, if it wasn't for one woman, one woman I never saw again, I'd not be here now."

He continued to look at me without saying a word.

"I'd moped in my flat for weeks then one day I couldn't take the guilt anymore. I was going to find somewhere high, throw myself off, end it all. On my way I bumped into someone. A tall lady, blonde hair, in her forties. And I don't know how she knew or why she chose to say anything but she grabbed my arm and told me not to do it. Life was precious, I should give it a second chance. That no mistake was bad enough to feel that amount of guilt.

"I continued walking but ended up making a circuit of my local area. I went home and started looking for a new job. It was her words—it was the kindness of that stranger that saved my life."

Xander's gaze softened, I didn't know why.

"I was determined to look only for work where I could be a positive influence. That's how I ended up at *Good Manors*. I've changed. I only do things that positively impact on people now. I never give a bad review. A starkly truthful review sometimes, but I'm never mean. I couldn't be. I'd never sell anything to a tabloid, I couldn't. I made a mistake, a big, stupid, idiotic mistake that ended in someone taking his own life. And then I made another mistake by not telling you who I was. But I was scared. I love my job and if I couldn't have reviewed Mallard's maybe I'd have been let go. Maxine is like that. She accepts nothing less than the best. And I didn't want you to hate me. I didn't want you to send me away."

"What did the blonde woman look like?" Xander asked and I wondered if he'd really been listening to me.

"Oh, she was pretty tall, elegant. Had a lovely navy blue suit on with a pretty red rose brooch. It sparkled so much I thought it had to be rubies. She had lovely blue eyes too, almost gray. I wonder sometimes if she was an angel."

"Yeah, she was." Xander smiled and walked toward me. "That was my mother."

Chapter Twenty-Two

Xander Patrick

"Your mother? Are you sure?" She shook her head in disbelief.

"Yeah, yeah, I'm sure. I remember it clear as day. She'd gone into town to talk to the bank manager, to try and get a loan. We'd decided we were going to try to make Mallard's into a viable visitor attraction. She was really nervous, because you know, it wasn't long after Father died and she'd never dealt with that kind of stuff before and I was too young to do it for her." I smiled. "I'd wanted to go with her but she'd left me in charge of the workmen at the Hall. I was twelve and completely in over my head but I did my best because Mum was depending on me.

"When she came back she told me how nervous she'd been and how she nearly turned back, called it all off but then she met a young girl with dark eyes and a haunted look. She said she knew, just knew, the poor thing was going to do something silly so Mum stopped her, told her not to. That no mistake was that bad. Not to feel guilty. That meeting and the realization in the girl's eyes gave her the strength to continue on to the bank, to get the loan and make Mallard's what it is now."

"That girl...was me?" She quickly vibrated her head from side to side and squinted like she was trying to see exactly what I was saying.

"Yes, that girl was you. Mum wore her favorite navy blue suit that day, and the rose broach with the rubies. She sold it after her meeting at the bank. It kept us going until the loan money came in, that's why I remember it. "

India's hand flew to her mouth and tears sprang to her eyes.

"It was your mum. It was Lord Mallard's wife. And she... She...."

India didn't need to finish her sentence. My mum saved her life. Told her no mistake was worth feeling that guilty about, gave her the strength to go on. Maybe that was the message I should also give her. I stepped closer and wrapped my arms around her. She buried her face into my shoulder and wept.

I laid my cheek against her hair and let the tears drip down. I wasn't sure I believed in destiny or fate or any of that but at that moment it did seem like something out there in the universe wanted us to be together.

"I'm so sorry, Xander," she sobbed. "So very sorry."

"Shh." I kissed the top of her head. "It doesn't matter now."

"But it does matter." She lifted her head and pushed back until just my hands rested on her elbow. "It does matter, Xander. I wronged you and your family and—"

"And what? India, you've rescued me. You've rescued Mallard's. We can barely keep up with the visitors now. You helped Harriet give birth, you helped us find Grace."

"It doesn't change what I did." She sighed.

"No, but we all make mistakes, India, and you didn't kill him. He did that himself. He wasn't a saint."

"But no one deserves—"

"India, shut up and let me kiss you."

She was stunned. I took advantage and kissed her and pushed all emotion inside me through that bridge between us, through our kiss, to show her just how much I needed her.

"Oh, Xander," she groaned. "I've missed you."

"Missed you too," I whispered against her ear, "so much."

"I can't believe this is real."

"It is," I replied. "Now, India Grace, come with me. We have a lot of catching up to do."

"Where are we going?" she asked as I pulled her down the corridor beside me.

"My room," I replied.

"Oh," she blurted.

We hurried along until we reached my room. I threw open the door then pushed it closed quickly, locked it.

"Xander, are you sure—?"

"Very." I nodded. It still hurt when I thought about it, the betrayal, the way she'd lied, but I wanted her.

"I don't think I can take it if we—"

I kissed her again, tried to show her how much I wanted her.

"If you don't want me, tell me." I stepped back and licked my lips. "But I want you."

"I want you too." She gasped and pushed her body against mine, tipping her head for a kiss.

I took her lips and all her whirling emotions and wrapped her up in my arms. I stilled my brain and let my body take control. Pulled off her T-shirt as she scrabbled to undo my overalls. Pinged open her bra when she opened the last button. We worked to get my arms out of the overalls. We were both determined to lose all the barriers between us and stripped off the rest of our clothes quickly, kissing and stroking each other when we could.

I didn't think, I felt. I felt her soft skin, the kiss of her eyelashes against my cheek, the wash of her tears splashing down on my chest as I held her so tightly. We rolled around on the bed, her curves surrounding me, pulling me in. She was so soft and giving. I felt alive again being with her.

We went together so well. Our movements mirrored each other. She read my desire and I realized hers—they were one and the same. I drowned my sorrows with the juices of her pussy. I drank and sucked and licked her to a screaming orgasm, and only then did I kneel between her thighs. She pulled me close to her, dug her nails into my back as I fucked her. It wasn't pretty, soft or sweet. I just sated my urge, I needed her so much.

In the aftermath, we lay together panting, snuggled close.

We didn't speak and eventually India fell asleep. I cuddled her to me and looked up at the ceiling.

It was then that doubts that I'd held back in the rush of emotion raised their heads. Could I forgive her? I thought I already had. I'd mourned my father's passing years ago. I was over that. I accepted that she'd made a mistake. It concerned me that she'd kept it quiet all that time, hadn't told me. What else could she be hiding?

Yeah, Mum had saved her life, but she'd hated journalists all her life long. Would she really approve of me and India if she were still around? My heart throbbed. I missed that woman every day. She had always helped me work out what to do.

I tried to allay my fears and think about life going forward. Surely it would be so much better with India by my side. But what would happen if the tabloids got a hold of the story? *India Grace, the photographer who sent Lord Mallard into an unstoppable death spiral, and his son shacked up together.* They would have a field day. What if that impacted Mallard's? People might not come. They were weird like that. One whiff of scandal and the place would be derelict.

It was lucky that we'd managed to keep the shop debacle under wraps, really. There was a little bit in the local rag about the lambnapping but for legal reasons they'd not been able to name Gerald in it anyway.

But this, this would affect the Hall. What if people thought India's positive review was just about appeasing her guilt or trying to get into bed with me? I'd be tarnished with the same reputation my dad had, and that had ruined Mallard's. I couldn't do something that would repeat that.

Mum gave her life to see it thrive.

So within half an hour I'd gone from not caring and wanting India in my life forever to the complete opposite. It would be difficult to live without her but I was certain it was the best thing to do for the long-term success of Mallard's. And Mallard's was my life. I could live with being miserable for a while if it meant Mallard's would be a success.

I pulled away from India's naked form, covered her with a blanket and left her sleeping. I pulled on my discarded T-shirt and underpants then sat down on the chair in the corner. I grabbed a notebook and scribbled down a note for India.

India,

I'm sorry, I can't do this. I thought I could but I can't. I have forgiven you for what you did to Dad but I'm struggling to forget how long you lied to me. I'm not sure we should really be together. I think it would be bad for us and for Mallard's.

I know I got your hopes up only to dash them. I appreciate you coming here to tell me your side of the story and I do think that it is beautiful that my mum saved your life. And that you, in turn, saved Grace and Harriet and the business. I think we're even.

Please don't try to find me once you read this. I'm not strong enough to resist your beauty. I'm weak and stupid and I don't want to hurt you again. You have an amazing career ahead of you. Go, enjoy, live life.

Xander

I pondered for ages how to sign off and in the end I chickened out, just signing my name with no kind of 'love' or 'yours sincerely' or anything like that.

I left the note on top of India's clothes, looked longingly at her peaceful form then tiptoed out. A little way up the corridor, I bumped into Mary.

"Oh, India was here, looking for you. Did she find you?"

"Yes, Mary." I smiled.

"Oh good, good." She wanted more. I could see it written all over her face. I loved Mary to bits but she was an awful gossip so I wasn't going to say another word.

"I have heard great things about Harry." Mary obviously realized I wasn't going to play ball and had moved on to the next item of her agenda. "There have been some really positive feedback forms left too. Apparently he's a great tour guide."

"Who'd have thought?" I laughed. Harry was a quiet guy but apparently talking about Mallard's history brought him out of his shell.

"I know. Crazy, isn't it? We put an ad in the local paper for a new gardener. We've promoted Mark to head gardener, remember, but he needs an assistant."

"Good, let me know when we're looking to hold interviews."

"Sure, will do." She nodded, looked me up and down then sighed. "Xander, I can read you like a well-thumbed woman's magazine in a doctor's office. What's the matter?"

"Nothing," I protested, a little high-pitched to be completely convincing.

"Well, if you don't want to talk about it, that's fine, I guess." She humphed and shrugged. "But don't hold it in forever. It's not healthy and it makes you a right grumpy sod."

I laughed and shook my head.

"I promise I won't be grumpy, Mary. Thanks."

"I suppose that'll have to do for now. Okay then, boss. See you round."

I went back to the library, gathered my tools then hid them away in the secret passage for later. It was time to go check on my sheep. Grace was less lamb and more like her mum, and both were due for shearing. Their wool would earn me a pretty penny. They would also be the first animals in my rare breeds stable. I was going to develop an area of the farm for visitors to come and meet and pet the animals, breeds close to passing into obscurity.

That and the library were my next expansion plans and I was sure both would work wonders for Mallard's, even if they ran me into the ground first.

When I finally walked back to the Hall, India's car was gone. I wasn't sure if I was relieved or upset that she'd gone without even trying to change my mind. When I reached my room, there was a note left on the bed for me.

Xander,
I'm sorry. I should never have come. Least now I know I could never have replaced the bricks and mortar you live in at the center of your heart. I thought I'd fallen in love with you. Now I know that it was just a mirage. I wish you and Mallard's all the best.
India

I sat on my bed and stared at the wall.

What a mess, what a stupid mess. I shouldn't have let her get to me in the first place.

From that moment on I tried to push India from my mind, but it didn't work. She haunted me, every day and every night. Everywhere I went in the Hall she followed me. As I oversaw the renovation of the library I saw her, when I purchased animals I thought of her veterinary skills. When I was in bed I remembered rolling around it with her. Even when I slept I saw her, flogged her, spanked her arse. She followed me day and night and drove me insane.

In the end I decided the only way to escape was to put the Hall on the market and move. I had to escape the memory of her. I loved Mallard Hall, it had been my life's work, but every inch of the place reminded me of her and it drove me to distraction. I made a list of ways to eradicate her memory and there ended up being two options. Knock the manor down and rebuild it or leave. No amount of new wallpaper or different furniture would stop me remembering the good times we'd had together. A new start, a new life in a completely different place was the only way to deal with it and keep Mallard's intact. I had my eye on a run-down mansion in Scotland. A little place I could do up and run like an upmarket B&B. Maybe there I could become a new man. A man not held down by memories and the past.

Chapter Twenty-Three

India Grace

"Hey, India," Brendan said, "have you seen that Mallard's is up for sale?"

"Is it?" I asked. "Really?"

"Yeah, they sent the specs over for me to include in the real estate listings this month."

"No, I don't believe it. Xander was totally dedicated to that place."

Brendan shrugged. "Well, the listing will be in the magazine. Check it out if you don't believe me."

My mind raced. Why would Xander put the Hall on the market?

When I got home, I looked it up online and sure enough I found several mentions of his listing. Including a newly renovated library and a rare breeds farm for visitors, Mallard's was still a successful, going concern. So why on earth was Xander selling up?

It irked me—I didn't sleep well and the next day I couldn't settle to writing. It was wrong. Mallard Hall should belong to a Mallard. Should belong to Xander. Not anyone else. What had happened to make him sell?

I'd worked really hard to eliminate the man from my life. I'd built up a lot of hate for him over the months since we'd last seen each other but I just couldn't shake the wrongness of this piece of news. In the end I jumped into my car and pointed it toward Mallard's.

I still didn't know what I thought I could do. He'd made it quite clear that my opinion didn't matter to him, that I didn't matter to him full stop. I couldn't let him do it. Whatever his motivation was, it had to be wrong. He'd put so much into Mallard's, it would be a travesty to let him leave.

When I arrived it was late in the day, the shop was shut and the main entrance barred. I went round the back and rang the bell.

"God, India, what are you doing here?" Jenny answered the door and threw her arms around me.

"I've come to see Xander."

"Yeah, of course. He's in the office. I think he's had an offer on the place. Some Arabian chap looked round it today."

"Jenny, I can't believe he's selling."

"I know." She sighed. "But he's insisting they take on the existing staff when they buy. That's something I guess."

I didn't want to take away her comfort blanket but an agreement like that needed to be on paper to mean anything, and even then once any stated term was up they'd be out on their arses.

"I can find my way to the office from here—you get back to what you were doing."

"Okay, will do. Oh, it's nice to see you. Make sure you call in on Mary before you go."

"I will do," I shouted after her then resumed the walk to the office. Outside, I took a deep breath then knocked on the door.

"Come in!" he yelled.

His voice made my stomach flip over and over again like a clockwork dog.

"What do you want, Mary? I'm really very busy. I need to get this contract sorted."

"Hi, Xander."

He looked up and the full glare of his piercing eyes rested on me. "India?" He gasped. "What are you doing here?"

"I saw that Mallard's was on the market," I replied. He was wearing his black suit, a lightly pinstriped blue shirt beneath it, opened so I could see glimpses of his chest hair.

"Yeah, looks like I've got a buyer."

"Why?" I asked. "That's why I'm here. It doesn't make sense to me." I stopped beside his desk and waited for his answer.

"It's not really any of your business." He bristled.

"No, you're right, it isn't. But—stupidly it seems—I thought you might be in trouble of some sort. I wanted to help."

"No trouble, it's time I left."

"But why, Xander, why? You gave up on me for this place. Now you're leaving Mallard's. Is that how little you thought of me?"

"How can you ask that?" he growled. "Were you really that blind?"

"Did you see the note you left me? I've read it every day since. Every fucking day, and I see the indifference in your words. I thought I meant something to you. I broke my heart over you, Xander. Then you offered me a glimpse of hope only to break it all over again. Do you hate me that much?" My voice caught and I gulped back threatening tears.

"No," Xander snapped, pushing back his chair and standing. "No, it's because I loved you far too much, India. I can see you in every little last bit of this place. There isn't a room I can go to where I don't think of you and what I lost, okay? So that's why I'm going. Trying to find some peace. From you."

"Me?" I shook my head. "I thought you didn't feel anything for me. I thought you used me."

"No." He sighed. "No, I loved you, India."

"Then why did you push me away?" What was he saying? I couldn't work it out. Everything I thought was truth seemed to be crumbling around me.

"I was scared. Scared that the media would get a hold of the story and it'd ruin Mallard's."

"Story, what story?"

"Me and you. You being the ruin of my father. Maybe they'd see your article as a way of appeasing your guilt, not truth," Xander shouted.

"And who bloody cares? Not the people who visit here anyway. You sent me that nasty fucking letter because you just blew things out of proportion?" I growled, hate and disbelief raging inside.

"I wanted a future with you, India. I couldn't see it working. It hurt, so I pushed you away."

"Xander." I cupped his chin in my hand. "I loved you so much. I'd have done anything for you if you'd asked. Including leaving. Which I did. I turned my love to hate. I've actively despised you for months. Now you're going to sacrifice your legacy, the love of your life because of me. I can't let you do that."

"India." He rested his large hand over mine. "Oh, India. I know it sounds stupid but your memory is driving me wild. I loved you too and every step I take in this house reminds me of you. I don't want to live here without you."

"Xander," I whispered, barely believing what I was about to say. "What if we try to love again?"

He shook his head, his hands vibrated, his toes tapped. He looked to be fighting with himself. He exhaled but before he could say a word I jumped in.

"Hear me out. I've hated you but only because I loved you. Yeah, there might be a bit of media backlash to us getting together, if someone can be arsed digging to find out that link to our past. But what does it really matter? They don't say no publicity is bad publicity for no reason, you know." It was strange. The hate melted so quickly, it was like it was just a coating, protecting the love inside until I could use it again.

"Do you think?" he asked. "It can't be that simple, can it?"

I looked him straight in the eye, confronted the stare that had haunted my dreams.

"Yes, I do," I said. "Don't leave Mallard's, Xander. Don't leave me."

"India." He gasped and pulled me into his embrace, pressing his lips to mine.

I could feel his heart pounding, echoing my own, the heat of his body, the familiar feel of his arms around me. Oh, I'd missed it so much. All through the journey to Mallard's I'd been denying to myself the true reason I had gone. It wasn't about Mallard's at all. It was about me and him. I couldn't let him go.

"I don't want to go," Xander said when we parted to breathe. "I never wanted to go. I wanted you, India, and I was so stupid."

"Shh." I pressed my finger to his lips. "That's the past now, let's forget it. This moment is what matters. Are you going to stay at Mallard's?"

He looked at me and nodded. I moved my finger so he could speak.

"Yes, I am."

"Good." I smiled.

"Now I need to ask you a question." His arms were still round me and we were pressed so closely together I could feel he was aroused. "Will you stay here with me?"

"Stay here?" I questioned. "I'd love to, but I don't know if it could work."

"You don't work from an office, do you?" Xander asked.

"No, I'm kinda independent. Only go in for weekly team meetings, really."

"Well, a once a week trip into the city isn't hard to do."

"But we'd be together, you know, all the time." I didn't want us fighting again.

"Not when you're doing your work. It'll only be the between times."

He was making it really hard to say no and I realized after a while that I didn't want to.

"Okay then, I'll stay with you, Xander. I'll have to work it out with work and stuff but yes, I will."

"Good," he replied. "Now, India, one last question."

"Yes?"

"Can I fuck you?"

I gasped in fake affront.

"What a question to ask a lady!"

He nuzzled my neck again, kissed the dip by my collarbone and made me moan. "Please?" he purred, the vibration making my skin tingle.

"Well, since you asked so nicely."

He grabbed me and pushed me back onto his desk until I was sitting, thighs spread around him, feet dangling a few inches off the ground. He stepped back.

"Stay there." He smiled, threw off his jacket and walked away from me.

A few moments later I heard the lock on the door click and a little after that he was back, bare chested. "Now, let's even this up."

He lifted my bright green T-shirt at the front and pulled it up and over my head. Next he released the clasp of my bra and brought us close until our warm chests rubbed together and I couldn't help moaning.

He ran his strong hands down my back, making me shiver, then skimmed them round the top of my jeans. Xander pressed his lips to mine as he undid the button and zip. I lifted up so he could drag the jeans away from me and he efficiently removed my knickers at the same time, stroking them down my legs and pulling them off my feet with my shoes.

He moved in and I lovingly caressed his chest, peppered it with kisses while he removed his own trousers and underwear. He stepped closer so I could wrap my thighs around him. I dragged him in for a kiss. It scorched my lips and set my whole body on fire.

"Fuck," he groaned, and I angled myself so I could rub my wet pussy up and down his cock. "That feels good."

"Mm-hm," was all the reply I could muster. I couldn't think straight, his cock tip kissed my clit and I bucked with pleasure.

"I need to be inside you," he whispered against my ear.

I curved back, resting my hands on the desk, tipping my pelvis so he could push himself into me. Once he was inside, he cupped my breasts and leaned forward to kiss them. He licked and nibbled at my nipple, and when I was groaning for more he bit down. I moaned and remembered how cruelly exciting he could be. I loved it and wanted more.

"Fuck," I cried. He used his fingers to pluck each nipple, pulling them tight and making my cunt squeeze around him.

He groaned in delight, my pain heightening my pleasure. I wondered if my pain worked the same way for him too.

He gathered me in his arms and snuggled my body to his. His hot chest pressed against my breasts, the hard planes of him dug into my soft curves and made my sensitive nipples ache. We clung to each other, kissing and moaning. I ran my hands into his hair and he scratched his nails down my back. I wanted him to mark me, to make me his so we would never be parted again.

I crashed to orgasm quickly, his pelvis rubbing against my clit over and over, and moments later, as we cuddled so tightly, he came too, groaning into my mouth through our kiss. We panted and moaned, our orgasms melting into contentment. It was a fast and furious coupling but fulfilling. I held onto him, I didn't want to let go. I didn't want the dream to end.

"I love you, India," he whispered into my ear. "Don't ever leave me."

"I love you too," I replied, lifting my head to look into his eyes. "I won't ever go. My home is here with you, always."

"Good." He kissed my forehead. "Oh so good."

We finally parted. Xander rang the estate agent and told them he was no longer selling Mallard's as I dressed.

"Are you all right?" he asked, buttoning up his shirt.

"Yes," I replied. "I'm fine, just finding it all a little hard to believe."

"I can pinch you again to prove it is if you like."

My nipples puckered in remembered pain.

"No, no, I'm okay for now." I laughed. "This will all be the same in the morning, won't it, Xander? You won't change your mind?"

"No, I won't." He pulled me into his embrace. "I was a fool, India, and to have you back here is a miracle, I'm not going to waste it."

"Good." I sighed. "I love it here, I love you."

"I love you too, India. And one day I want you to be my Lady Mallard."

"Really?"

He nodded, his chin patting the top of my head.

"Yes, I thought I might be pushing my luck proposing when we'd only just got back together but when I'm with you, in you, surrounded by you, I know I've found my soul mate."

Tipping back my head, I looked deep into his eyes.

"Lord Mallard, you are my world and I would love to be your lady."

"To honor and obey?" he asked with a wicked glint in his eye.

"Yes, Sir, of course."

"Good." He kissed me so sweetly, I was alive with happiness. "Now I suppose I need to go shopping for a ring and a collar."

"Perfect," I purred and kissed him again. Sometimes fairy-tale endings do become true.

About the Author

Victoria Blisse is a mother, wife, Christian, Manchester United fan and award winning erotica author. She is also the editor of several Bigger Briefs collections, and the co-editor of the fabulous Smut Alfresco and Smut in the City and Smut by the Sea Anthologies.

She is equally at home behind a laptop or a cooker (She is TEB's resident 'Naked Chef') and she loves to create stories, poems, cakes and biscuits that make people happy. She was born near Manchester, England and her northern English quirkiness shows through in all of her stories. Passion, love and laughter fill her works, just as they fill her busy life.

Victoria Blisse loves to hear from readers. You can find her contact information, website and author biography at http://www.totallybound.com.

TOTALLY
BOUND
Home of Erotic Romance

www.ingramcontent.com/pod-product-compliance
Lightning Source LLC
Chambersburg PA
CBHW030135180626
46812CB00002B/697

* 9 7 8 1 7 8 4 3 0 7 8 2 0 *